Coming Out

Also by Danielle Steel

THE HOUSE
TOXIC BACHELORS
MIRACLE
IMPOSSIBLE
ECHOES
SECOND CHANCE
RANSOM
SAFE HARBOUR
JOHNNY ANGEL
DATING GAME
ANSWERED PRAYERS
SUNSET IN ST. TROPEZ
THE COTTAGE
THE KISS
LEAP OF FAITH
LONE EAGLE
JOURNEY
THE HOUSE ON HOPE STREET
THE WEDDING
IRRESISTIBLE FORCES
GRANNY DAN
BITTERSWEET
MIRROR IMAGE
HIS BRIGHT LIGHT: *The Story of Nick Traina*
THE KLONE AND I
THE LONG ROAD HOME
THE GHOST
SPECIAL DELIVERY
THE RANCH
SILENT HONOR
MALICE
FIVE DAYS IN PARIS
LIGHTNING
WINGS
THE GIFT
ACCIDENT
VANISHED
MIXED BLESSINGS
JEWELS
NO GREATER LOVE
HEARTBEAT
MESSAGE FROM NAM
DADDY
STAR
ZOYA
KALEIDOSCOPE
FINE THINGS
WANDERLUST
SECRETS
FAMILY ALBUM
FULL CIRCLE
CHANGES
THURSTON HOUSE
CROSSINGS
ONCE IN A LIFETIME
A PERFECT STRANGER
REMEMBRANCE
PALOMINO
LOVE: POEMS
THE RING
LOVING
TO LOVE AGAIN
SUMMER'S END
SEASON OF PASSION
THE PROMISE
NOW AND FOREVER
PASSION'S PROMISE
GOING HOME

DANIELLE STEEL

COMING OUT

DOUBLEDAY LARGE PRINT HOME LIBRARY EDITION

Delacorte Press

This Large Print Edition, prepared especially for Doubleday Large Print Home Library, contains the complete, unabridged text of the original Publisher's Edition.

COMING OUT
A Delacorte Book / July 2006

Published by Bantam Dell
A Division of Random House, Inc.
New York, New York

This is a work of fiction. Names, characters, places, and incidents either are the product of the author's imagination or are used fictitiously. Any resemblance to actual persons, living or dead, events, or locales is entirely coincidental.

ISBN-10: 0-7394-6882-0
ISBN-13: 978-0-7394-6882-1

Printed in the United States of America
Published simultaneously in Canada

This Large Print Book carries the Seal of Approval of N.A.V.H.

To my wonderful and very special children:
Beatrix, Trevor, Todd, Nick,
Samantha, Victoria, Vanessa,
Maxx, and Zara,
for all their courage and grace
as they grow up.
For the wisdom, laughter, and love
they share with me so lavishly.
With my thanks for all you have taught me,
about what matters in life, and
the precious times we share. May you be
forever blessed. With all my heart and love,

Mom/d.s.

Proverbs 31

10: Who can find a virtuous woman? For her price is far above rubies.

11: The heart of her husband doth safely trust in her. . . .

12: She will do him good and not evil all the days of her life.

13: . . . She worketh willingly with her hands.

14: . . . She bringeth her food from afar.

15: She riseth while it is yet night, and giveth meat to her household. . . .

16: She considereth a field and buyeth it: with the fruit of her hands she planteth a vineyard.

18: . . . her candle goeth not out by night.

20: She stretcheth out her hand to the poor; yea, she reacheth forth her hands to the needy.

25: Strength and honor are her clothing; and she shall rejoice in time to come.

26: She openeth her mouth with wisdom; and in her tongue is the law of kindness.

27: She looketh well to the ways of her household, and eateth not the bread of idleness.

28: Her children arise up and call her blessed; her husband also praiseth her.

29: Many daughters have done virtuously, but thou excellest them all.

31: Give her of the fruit of her hands; and let her own works praise her in the gates.

Coming Out

Chapter 1

Olympia Crawford Rubinstein was whizzing around her kitchen on a sunny May morning, in the brownstone she shared with her family on Jane Street in New York, near the old meat-packing district of the West Village. It had long since become a fashionable neighborhood of mostly modern apartment buildings with doormen, and old renovated brownstones. Olympia was fixing lunch for her five-year-old son, Max. The school bus was due to drop him off in a few minutes. He was in kindergarten at Dalton, and Friday was a half day for him. She always took Fridays off to spend them with him. Although Olympia had three older children from her first marriage, Max was Olympia and Harry's only child.

Olympia and Harry had restored the house six years before, when she was pregnant with Max. Before that, they had lived in her Park Avenue apartment, which she had previously shared with her three children after her divorce. And then Harry joined them. She had met Harry Rubinstein a year after her divorce. And now, she and Harry had been married for thirteen years. They had waited eight years to have Max, and his parents and siblings adored him. He was a loving, funny, happy child.

Olympia was a partner in a booming law practice, specializing in civil rights issues and class action lawsuits. Her favorite cases, and what she specialized in, were those that involved discrimination against or some form of abuse of children. She had made a name for herself in her field. She had gone to law school after her divorce, fifteen years before, and married Harry two years later. He had been one of her law professors at Columbia Law School, and was now a judge on the federal court of appeals. He had recently been considered for a seat on the Supreme Court. In the end, they hadn't appointed him, but he'd come close, and she and Harry both hoped that the next time a vacancy came up, he would get it.

She and Harry shared all the same beliefs, values, and passions—even though they came from very different backgrounds. He came from an Orthodox Jewish home, and both his parents had been Holocaust survivors as children. His mother had gone to Dachau from Munich at ten, and lost her entire family. His father had been one of the few survivors of Auschwitz, and they met in Israel later. They had married as teenagers, moved to London, and from there to the States. Both had lost their entire families, and their only son had become the focus of all their energies, dreams, and hopes. They had worked like slaves all their lives to give him an education, his father as a tailor and his mother as a seamstress, working in the sweatshops of the Lower East Side, and eventually on Seventh Avenue in what was later referred to as the garment district. His father had died just after Harry and Olympia married. Harry's greatest regret was that his father hadn't known Max. Harry's mother, Frieda, was a strong, intelligent, loving woman of seventy-six, who thought her son was a genius, and her grandson a prodigy.

Olympia had converted from her staunch Episcopalian background to Judaism when she married Harry. They attended a Reform synagogue, and Olympia said the prayers for Shabbat every Friday night, and lit the candles, which never failed to touch Harry. There was no doubt in Harry's mind, or even his mother's, that Olympia was a fantastic woman, a great mother to all her children, a terrific attorney, and a wonderful wife. Like Olympia, Harry had been married before, but he had no other children. Olympia was turning forty-five in July, and Harry was fifty-three. They were well matched in all ways, though their backgrounds couldn't have been more different. Even physically, they were an interesting and complementary combination. Her hair was blond, her eyes were blue; he was dark, with dark brown eyes; she was tiny; he was a huge teddy bear of a man, with a quick smile and an easygoing disposition. Olympia was shy and serious, though prone to easy laughter, especially when it was provoked by Harry or her children. She was a remarkably dutiful and loving daughter-in-law to Harry's mother, Frieda.

Olympia's background was entirely different from Harry's. The Crawfords were an illustrious and extremely social New York family, whose blue-blooded ancestors had intermarried with Astors and Vanderbilts for generations. Buildings and academic institutions were named after them, and theirs had been one of the largest "cottages" in Newport, Rhode Island, where they spent the summers. The family fortune had dwindled to next to nothing by the time her parents died when she was in college, and she had been forced to sell the "cottage" and surrounding estate to pay their debts and taxes. Her father had never really worked, and as one of her distant relatives had said after he died, "he had a small fortune, he had made it from a large one." By the time she cleaned up all their debts and sold their property, there was simply no money, just rivers of blue blood and aristocratic connections. She had just enough left to pay for her education, and put a small nest egg away, which later paid for law school.

She married her college sweetheart, Chauncey Bedham Walker IV, six months after she graduated from Vassar, and he from Princeton. He had been charming, handsome, and fun-loving, the captain of the crew team, an expert horseman, played polo, and when they met, Olympia was understandably dazzled by him. Olympia was head over heels in love with him, and didn't give a damn about his family's enormous fortune. She was totally in love with Chauncey, enough so as not to notice that he drank too much, played constantly, had a roving eye, and spent far too much money. He went to work in his family's investment bank, and did anything he wanted, which eventually included going to work as seldom as possible, spending literally no time with her, and having random affairs with a multitude of women. By the time she knew what was happening, she and Chauncey had three children. Charlie came along two years after they were married, and his identical twin sisters, Virginia and Veronica, three years later. When she and Chauncey split up seven years after they married, Charlie was five, the twins two, and Olympia was twenty-nine years old. As soon as they separated, he quit his job at the bank, and went to live in Newport with his grandmother, the doyenne of Newport and Palm Beach society, and devoted himself to playing polo and chasing women.

A year later Chauncey married Felicia Weatherton, who was the perfect mate for him. They built a house on his grandmother's estate, which he ultimately inherited, filled her stables with new horses, and had three daughters in four years. A year after Chauncey married Felicia, Olympia married Harry Rubinstein, which Chauncey found not only ridiculous but appalling. He was rendered speechless when their son, Charlie, told him his mother had converted to the Jewish faith. He had been equally shocked earlier when Olympia enrolled in law school, all of which proved to him, as Olympia had figured out long before, that despite the similarity of their ancestry, she and Chauncey had absolutely nothing in common, and never would. As she grew older, the ideas that had seemed normal to her in her youth appalled her. Almost all of Chauncey's values, or lack of them, were anathema to her.

The fifteen years since their divorce had been years of erratic truce, and occasional minor warfare, usually over money. He supported their three children decently, though not generously. Despite what he had inherited from his family, Chauncey was stingy with his first family, and far more generous with his second wife and their children. To add insult to injury, he had forced Olympia to agree that she would never urge their children to become Jewish. It wasn't an issue anyway. She had no intention of doing so. Olympia's conversion was a private, personal decision between her and Harry. Chauncey was unabashedly anti-Semitic. Harry thought Olympia's first husband was pompous, arrogant, and useless. Other than the fact that he was her children's father and she had loved him when she married him, for the past fifteen years, Olympia found it impossible to defend him. Prejudice was Chauncey's middle name. There was absolutely nothing politically correct about him or Felicia, and Harry loathed him. They represented everything he detested, and he could never understand how Olympia had tolerated him for ten minutes, let alone seven years of marriage. People like Chauncey and Felicia, and the whole hierarchy of Newport society, and all it stood for, were a mystery to Harry. He wanted to know nothing about it, and Olympia's occasional explanations were wasted on him.

Harry adored Olympia, her three children, and their son, Max. And in some ways, her daughter Veronica seemed more like Harry's daughter than Chauncey's. They shared all of the same extremely liberal, socially responsible ideas. Virginia, her twin, was much more of a throwback to their Newport ancestry, and was far more frivolous than her twin sister. Charlie, their older brother, was at Dartmouth, studying theology and threatening to become a minister. Max was a being unto himself, a wise old soul, who his grandmother swore was just like her own father, who had been a rabbi in Germany before being sent to Dachau, where he had helped as many people as he could before he was exterminated along with the rest of her family.

The stories of Frieda's childhood and lost loved ones always made Olympia weep. Frieda Rubinstein had a number tattooed on the inside of her left wrist, which was a sobering reminder of the childhood the Nazis had stolen from her. Because of it, she had worn long sleeves all her life, and still did. Olympia frequently bought beautiful silk blouses and long-sleeved sweaters for her. There was a powerful bond of love and respect between the two women, which continued to deepen over the years.

Olympia heard the mail being pushed through the slot in the front door, went to get it, and tossed it on the kitchen table as she finished making Max's lunch. With perfect timing, she heard the doorbell ring at almost precisely the same instant. Max was home from school, and she was looking forward to spending the afternoon with him. Their Fridays together were always special. Olympia knew she had the best of both worlds, a career she loved and that satisfied her, and a family that was the hub and core of her emotional existence. Each seemed to enhance and complement the other.

Olympia was taking Max to soccer practice that afternoon. She loved her time at home with her children. The twins would be home later that day, after their own after-school activities, which in their case included softball, tennis, swimming, and boys, whenever possible, particularly in Virginia's case. Veronica was more standoffish, shyer like her mother, and extremely particular about who she hung out with. Officially,

Virginia was more "popular," and Veronica the better student. Both girls had just been accepted at Brown for the fall, and were graduating in June.

Charlie had been accepted at Princeton, like his father, and three generations of Walkers before him, but had decided to go to Dartmouth instead, where he played ice hockey, and Olympia prayed that in spite of that he would graduate with teeth. He was due home for the summer in a week, and after visiting his father, stepmother, and three stepsisters in Newport, he was going to work at a camp in Colorado, teaching riding and taking care of horses. He had his father's love of equestrian pursuits, and was a skilled polo player, but preferred more informal aspects of the sport. Riding Western saddle all summer, and teaching kids, seemed like fun to him, and Olympia and Harry approved. The one thing Harry didn't think his stepson should do was waste a summer going to parties, like his father, in Newport. Harry thought Chauncey's whole lifestyle, and everyone in it, was a waste of time. And he was always pleased to notice that Charlie had a great deal more substance, and heart, than his father. He was a fine young man with a good head on his shoulders, a warm heart, and solid principles and beliefs.

The girls were going to Europe with friends as a graduation present, and Olympia, Harry, and Max were meeting them in Venice in August, and taking them on a driving trip through Umbria, to Lake Como, and into Switzerland, where Harry had distant relatives. Olympia was looking forward to the trip. Shortly after their return, she'd be taking the girls to Brown, and after that there would be only Max at home with her and Harry. The house already seemed too quiet to her these days, with Charlie gone. Having the girls leave too would be a real loss to her. Already now, with graduation and freedom imminent, the girls were almost never home. She had already missed Charlie terribly for the past three years. She was sorry that she and Harry hadn't decided to have more children after they had Max, but at nearly forty-five, she couldn't see herself starting with diapers and nursing schedules all over again. Those days were over for her, and having Max in their life, to bind them even closer together, seemed like an incredible gift.

Olympia ran to open the door as soon as she heard the bell, and there was Max, in all his five-year-old splendor, with a wide, happy grin, as he threw his arms around his mother's neck and hugged her, as he always did when he saw her. He was a happy, affectionate little boy.

"I had a *great* day, Mom!" he said enthusiastically. Max loved everything about life, his parents, his sisters, his brother whom he seldom saw but was crazy about, his grandmother, the sports he played, the movies he watched, the food his mother served him, his teachers, and his friends at school. "We had cupcakes for Jenny's birthday! They were chocolate with *sprinkles*!" He said it as though describing some rare and fabulous occurrence, although Olympia knew from volunteering in his kindergarten class that they had a birthday, with cupcakes and sprinkles, nearly every week. But to Max, every day, and the opportunities it offered, was wonderful and new.

"That sounds yummy." She beamed down at him, noticing the paint splattered all over his T-shirt. He dropped his sweatshirt on a chair, and she saw that his new tennis shoes were covered with paint, too.

Max was exuberant about everything he did. "Did you have art today?" she asked, as he settled into a chair at the big round kitchen table, where the family shared most of their meals. There was a pretty dining room with antiques she had inherited, but they only used it for the rare dinner parties they gave, and holidays like Christmas, Chanukah, Passover, and Thanksgiving. They celebrated both sets of holidays, both Christian and Jewish, in fairness to all their children. They wanted them to appreciate and respect both traditions. At first, Olympia's mother-in-law had been leery of that, but now she privately admitted that she enjoyed it, "for the children." The kitchen was the hub of the family wheel, and the nerve center of Olympia's operations. She had a small desk in the corner, with a computer, and a constantly precarious towering stack of papers, most of which dealt with the family. She had a small room upstairs, off their bedroom, which she used as a home office on Friday mornings, or occasionally at night, when she had a big case and brought work home with her. Most of the time, she tried to leave her law practice in the office, and focused on the children when she was home. But juggling both lives was a challenge at times. Harry and the older children admired her for how well she did it. Max didn't seem to notice. Whatever happened at home centered on the family, and not her legal work. She did her best to keep her two worlds separate. She rarely talked about her work with her children, unless they asked her. At home, she was more interested in talking about what they were doing. And she only had a sitter for Max for the hours she was at work, and not a minute longer. She loved being with him, and savored their time together.

"How did you know we had art today?" Max asked with interest, as he bit into the turkey sandwich she had made him. She did it just the way he liked it, with the right amount of mayonnaise, and a heap of his favorite potato chips. Her motherly skills were finely honed, and four star as far as Max was concerned. Her husband and three other children agreed. She was a good cook, a devoted mother, and made herself available to listen to their woes and solve their problems. She knew most of everything they did. She never divulged secrets, and gave fairly good advice about romantic problems, or so Virginia said. Veronica usually kept her crushes to herself, as Charlie did. He kept his own counsel about his relationships at college, just as he had when he was at home and in school. Charlie was a discreet and very private person and always had been. Harry said he was a "mensch," a man of integrity and great value. Sometimes he said Olympia was a "mensch," too, even though she was a woman. She knew it was a real compliment from him.

"I'm psychic," Olympia said in answer to Max's question, smiling into the dark brown eyes that were so much like his father's. His hair was so dark and shiny, it was almost blue. "Could be the paint on your shirt gave me a little hint." She didn't mention the shoes, and was sure he hadn't noticed. Max loved art, and like Charlie and Veronica, was an avid reader. Getting Virginia to do her reading assignments for school was a constant agony. As far as she was concerned, she had better things to do, like emailing her friends, talking on the phone, or watching MTV.

"What does sigh-sick mean again?" Max

looked puzzled for an instant, munching on a mouthful of chips, trying to remember the meaning of the word, which momentarily eluded him. He had a vocabulary well beyond his years.

"Psychic. It means I know what you're thinking," she explained, trying not to laugh at him. He was so damn cute.

"Yeah." He nodded, with a pensive look of admiration. "You always do. I guess that's what moms do." As far as he was concerned, she knew everything.

In Olympia's opinion, five was a great age. Whenever one of the girls told her what a monster she was, she still had Max to assure her that she could do no wrong. It was reassuring, and had been for the past couple of years, as the twins negotiated their way across the reefs and shoals of the teenage years. Particularly Virginia, who frequently disagreed with her mother, especially over things she wasn't allowed to do. Veronica's battles with her were over broader issues, and related more to the ills and injustices of the world.

Olympia felt that adolescent girls were a lot tougher to deal with than little boys in kindergarten, to say the least, or even their college junior brother, who had always been quiet, easy to get along with, and extremely reasonable. Charlie was the family negotiator and peacemaker, anxious to see that everyone got along, particularly the two branches of his extended family. He often saw both his mother's and his father's divergent points of view and ran interference between them, and when one of his sisters had an argument with their mother, it was Charlie who translated and negotiated the peace. Veronica was the acknowledged hothead and rebel, with some occasionally dicey political points of view, and Virginia was the fluff in the family, according to her twin sister. Virginia was usually more concerned with her looks and her love life than with deeper social or political issues. Veronica and Harry engaged in long, heated discussions at night, though usually of a strikingly similar opinion. Virginia marched to a different drummer than her sister, and spent hours poring over fashion magazines, or reading the gossip from Hollywood. She said she wanted to be a model or study acting. Veronica wanted to go to law school, like Harry and her mother, and was thinking about getting into politics after college.

Charlie hadn't figured out his future career yet, although he had only another year to do so. He was thinking of working at his father's family's investment bank right after college, or maybe studying for a year in Europe. Max was the family mascot who made everybody laugh in tense moments, and hug him whenever they laid eyes on him. All three of his older siblings adored him. Max had never met anyone who didn't like him, and he loved hanging out with his mother in the kitchen, lying on the floor just for the fun of it, drawing, or building things with blocks and Legos when she was on the phone. He was an easy child to amuse. He was almost always happy. He loved everything about his world, particularly the people in it.

Olympia handed him a Popsicle of real fruit juice and a cookie, while she flipped through the mail and poured herself a glass of iced tea. The weather had been warm for the past week, much to everyone's relief. It was finally spring. The warmer weather always took too long to come, as far as she was concerned. She hated the long eastern winters. By May, she was sick to death of warm coats, boots, snowsuits, mittens, and random snowstorms that came out of nowhere in April. She could hardly wait for the summer and their trip to Europe. She, Max, and Harry were going to the south of France for two weeks before they met the girls in Venice. By then, she'd be ready to escape the torrid summer heat in New York. Max was going to day camp until they left, where he could do art projects to his heart's content.

The remains of Max's grape juice Popsicle were dripping copiously down his chin and onto his shirt as he ate the cookie, while his mother glanced at the last piece of mail in the stack, and set down her iced tea. It was a large ecru-colored envelope that looked like a wedding invitation, and she couldn't imagine a single person they knew who might be getting married. She tore it open as Max began to hum a song he had learned in school, just as she saw that it was not a wedding invitation, but an invitation to a ball that was to take place in December, a very special ball. It was an invitation to the very elite debutante cotillion where she had come out herself at eighteen. It was called The Arches, after the elegant name and design of the Astor estate where it had originally been held. The estate had long since vanished, but the name had held over the years. Several of the city's most aristocratic families had organized the event in the late 1800s, when the purpose of a debutante ball had been to present young women to society, in order that they find husbands. In the hundred and twenty-five years since it was established, the purpose of the ball had inevitably changed. Young women now appeared in "society" long before they turned eighteen, and were no longer kept sequestered in schoolrooms. Now the ball was simply a fun and rather special social event, a rite of passage with no greater meaning or intent than to have a good time in so-called polite society, and the occasion to wear beautiful white dresses for one very special evening. It was a little bit like a wedding, and there were all sorts of archaic traditions associated with it—the curtsy the girls made as they entered the ballroom under a flowered archway, the first official dance with their fathers, always a dignified and graceful waltz, just as it had been in Olympia's day, and long before that.

It was an exciting moment in the lives of the young girls who were invited to make their debut at The Arches, and a memory most of them would cherish for the rest of their lives, provided no one got unduly drunk, had a fight with their escort, or had some ghastly accident to their dress before the presentation. Barring minor mishaps, it was a fun evening, and although admittedly somewhat old-fashioned and elitist, it did no one any harm. Olympia still cherished fond memories of her own debut, and had always assumed that her daughters would make their debut as well.

She had it in perspective, and knew how unimportant it was in the real scheme of things and world events, but also how much fun it could be for the girls who did it. It was a harmless even if frivolous landmark in a girl's life. She also knew that Chauncey expected the girls to do it, and would have been horrified if they didn't. Unlike Olympia, he thought coming out as a debutante *really* mattered, for all the wrong reasons. She was sure Veronica would grumble, and Virginia would be so excited she would want to go shopping for the dress within hours.

No one was expected to find husbands at debutante balls anymore, although now and then, and extremely rarely, a serious romance would be born that night, and then turn into marriage years later. But for the most part, the girls were escorted by cousins and brothers, or boys they had gone to school with. Asking a boyfriend to escort one seven months in advance was recognized as an invitation to trouble. At that age, on the eve of leaving for college, romances, no matter how hot and heavy they had been in June, usually didn't last till December. All the evening was about now was storing away one brief fairy tale memory for them to cherish and remember, and having a good time while they did it. Olympia was not surprised, but was nonetheless pleased that they had been asked. She had distanced herself so much from the official social scene in recent years that there had been the vague though unlikely possibility that the girls might have been dropped from the list. Both girls went to Spence, a school where many of the girls became debutantes, during the winter of their freshman year in college. There were other options, of course, and other debutante cotillions for slightly less blue-blooded girls. But The Arches had always been recognized as the ultimate deb ball in New York society.

Twenty-seven years earlier, Olympia had made her debut there herself, as had her mother and both grandmothers long before her, and her great-grandmothers once upon a time. It was a tradition she was going to enjoy sharing with her girls, no matter how much the world and society at large, or her own life, had changed in the meantime. Nowadays, women worked, people got married later than ever, and it was perfectly acceptable not to marry at all. And who one married had nothing to do with blue blood or society, as far as Olympia was concerned. All she wanted was for her daughters to marry good, solid, reliable, intelligent men who treated them well. Preferably, a man like Harry, and not their father. Now, more than anything, coming out was just an excuse to look lovely, and wear long white gloves and a beautiful white evening gown, often the first one the girls presented had ever worn. It was going to be fun helping Veronica and Virginia pick their dresses, particularly as she knew the choices the girls would make would be so different, as they always were. Having twins come out at The Arches was going to be double the fun for her. She sat staring dreamily at the invitation, with a gentle smile of memory and nostalgia on her face, as Max watched. He didn't often see his mom look like that. She felt almost like a young girl again, as memories of her own coming out flooded back to her, and Max observed her with interest. He could see that she was thinking of something that made her happy.

"What's that, Mom?" Max asked, wiping the grape juice off his chin with the back of his hand, and then brushing his hand against his jeans instead of his napkin.

"It's an invitation for your sisters," she said, slipping it back into the envelope, as she reminded herself to ask the committee for a duplicate invitation, so she could start an album for each girl, just like the one she had of her own debut, tucked away in the bookcase upstairs. One day it would be fun for them to have, to share with their own daughters. The twins had often looked at hers, when they were very little girls. Virginia had always said, at about Max's age, that their mom had looked like a fairy princess.

"Is that an invitation to a birthday party?" Max gazed at her, intrigued.

"To a coming-out ball," she explained. "It's a big party where you wear a beautiful white dress." She made it sound magical, like being Cinderella for one night at the ball, which in effect was what it was.

"What do you come out of?" Max asked, looking puzzled, as his mother smiled.

"That's a good question. You don't really come out of anything. Girls used to come out of their homes to find a husband. Now they just go to a party and have a good time."

"Are Ginny and Ver going to get married?" Max looked worried. He knew they were leaving for college, but getting married sounded like a much bigger deal to him.

"No, sweetheart. They're just going to get dressed up and go to the party. Daddy and I will go and watch. Daddy will dance with them, and so will their dad. Grandma Frieda will come, too, and then we'll all come home."

"That sounds boring," he said matter-of-factly. As far as Max was concerned, birthday parties were more fun. "Do I have to go?"

"Nope. Just the grown-ups." In fact, upholding the traditions of the event, no one younger than the correct age to be presented could come. Younger siblings were never allowed to attend. She suspected that one of them would want Charlie as an escort, and had no idea who the other twin would ask. Probably one of their friends. That was up to them. Her guess was that Veronica would corral Charlie, and Ginny would ask a friend. They had four weeks to respond, but there was no need to wait. She would send the check in the following week. The fee to participate was very small, and was donated to a designated charity, which benefited from the event. It was impossible to pay one's way in. It was not about money, it was about being asked, either as a legacy, as in the case of her girls, or as a result of one's blue-blooded ancestry and connections, which was also the case for her girls, although Olympia never traded on how social her family had been. It was just a fact of life for them, and something that was there, part of the furniture of their history and life. She never even thought about it. She was much prouder of her own family and accomplishments than of her family's "blue blood."

Max went upstairs to play in his room then. Harry called and said he'd be home late. He had a conference with two other judges after court that afternoon, and she never had a chance to tell him about the invitation. It was fun, but not that big a deal. She was going to tell him about it that night, when she told the girls. After that, she had to rush to take Max to soccer. They stopped to buy groceries afterward, and both girls were home by the time she and Max got back. Both girls were in a hurry to go out, each with a different set of friends. Harry came home even later than expected, and just as Olympia was cooking dinner, and the girls flew past on their way out, Max said he felt sick and suddenly threw up.

It was nine-thirty by the time she had settled him into bed, and he fell asleep after throwing up two more times. Harry said he was exhausted, and Olympia put their dinner in the fridge, and curled up on the couch next to him in the den. She had changed her own clothes twice, washed her hair, and looked exhausted, as Harry frowned over a mountain of papers he had brought home from the office for the weekend. He looked up at her with a warm smile, happy to see her, and to have a peaceful moment with her after a chaotic night.

"Welcome to real life." She smiled ruefully at him. "Sorry about dinner."

"I wasn't hungry anyway. Do you want me to fix you something?" he generously offered. He liked to cook, and was a far more creative chef than she. His specialties were omelets and Thai food, and he was always willing to cook for the family in a pinch, particularly if she was held up at the office during the week, which was rare for her, or in a crisis with the kids, like tonight with Max sick. They had a babysitter who came in for Max on the days she was working, and she and Harry always made an effort to come straight home from the office on those days. But she shook her head. She wasn't hungry either. "Is Max okay?"

"I think so. He ran around like crazy today at soccer, and took a couple of hits in the stomach. Either that or he's got a bug. I hope the others don't get sick." They were used to it, with four kids in the house, or even three now, flu bugs spread like wildfire, even to them. They had dealt with it for years. It had been a shock to Harry at first, but he had long since gotten used to it.

As it turned out, Max was still sick the next morning, and had a mild fever, which suggested to her that it was the flu, more likely than his exertions at soccer. Olympia went out to rent videos for him, while Harry kept him company, and Max slept for most of the afternoon. The girls were out for most of the weekend, and Ginny stayed over at a friend's. They were in the home stretch, the last few weeks of senior year, and there was lots of fun at hand.

It was Sunday night before everyone was home again. Max felt fine, and everyone was gathered around the kitchen table, while Harry and Veronica played cards with Max, Ginny read a magazine, and Olympia made dinner. She loved their family gatherings, and having them all underfoot while she cooked. It was why they had built a big cozy kitchen. For the first time in two days, she remembered the invitation that had arrived on Friday. She was just taking two chickens out of the oven, as she glanced toward the table, and mentioned it to all of them.

"Girls, you were invited to come out at The

Arches," she said casually, pulling a pan of baked potatoes out of the oven and setting them down on the kitchen counter, as Veronica looked up. She knew what The Arches was, and had already heard several girls at school mention it that week. All the invitations had been mailed, and all those who had been invited to come out knew it by then.

"How stupid," Veronica said with a look of disgust, as she dealt Max and Harry a fresh hand of cards. They were playing Go Fish, and so far Max had been winning, much to his delight. He loved beating his parents and older siblings at games.

"What did you just say, Mom?" Ginny asked, looking up with interest. They were both striking-looking blue-eyed blondes. Ginny wore her long hair straight, cascading over her shoulders, and was wearing a hint of makeup. Veronica wore hers in a braid, her face was scrubbed, and she had no need to wear makeup while playing cards with her stepfather and brother, or in fact most of the time. Their looks were identical, their styles noticeably different. It always helped identify them, which Harry had found useful over the years. If they had dressed identically and worn their hair the same way, he'd have been in trouble. In fact, without clothes, hairdos, or makeup to give one clues, their mother was the only one who could always tell them apart. Even Max got confused at times, and they teased him about it.

"I said, you were both invited to come out at The Arches in December. The invitation came this week." Olympia looked pleased for both of them, as she put butter in the baked potatoes, and carved the chicken. She had already made the salad.

"You don't expect us to do that, do you?" Veronica looked up in disapproval, as Olympia nodded, and Virginia smiled from ear to ear.

"How cool, Mom! I was afraid they wouldn't ask us. Everyone at school who's doing it got their invitations earlier this week." Their father had commented acidly years before that their mother's conversion to Judaism might get them blackballed.

"Yours came on Friday. I forgot to tell you after Max got sick," Olympia told her.

"When can we go shopping?" Ginny asked predictably, as their mother turned to them with a grin, and Veronica interrupted.

"Shopping? Are you crazy?" Veronica jumped up and stared at her sister with a look of outrage. "Are you telling me you're going to take part in that elitist discriminatory farce? For God's sake, Ginny, get your head out of your movie magazines for five minutes. They're not asking you to be queen for a day, or giving you an award here, they're asking you to discriminate against everyone who isn't a WASP and make a total ass of yourself, in a totally worthless, archaic, sexist tradition." She was on her feet and her eyes were blazing, as her sister and her mother stared at her in amazement. Olympia had expected her to grumble a little, but not to go completely insane.

"Let's not be too extreme. Nobody asked you to join a fascist movement, Veronica. It's only a coming-out party."

"What's the difference? Are there African Americans at The Arches? How about Jews? What about Hispanics or Asians? How can you be such a hypocrite, Mom? You're Jewish. You're married to Harry. If you make us do this, it's like a slap in his face." Veronica was beside herself with righteous indignation, as Virginia looked like she was about to cry.

"No one is slapping Harry's face. This is a perfectly innocuous debutante cotillion, where the two of you wear pretty white dresses, make your bow, and have a good time. And I have no idea who will be coming out with you, or what race they are. I haven't been to a deb ball in years."

"That's bullshit, Mom. You know this is a strictly WASP event, and all it's meant to do is shut people out. Nobody with a conscience should participate, and I'm not going to. I don't care what you say, or what Ginny does, I'm not going." Veronica was fighting mad as Virginia burst into tears.

"Calm down," Olympia said quietly and firmly, slightly unnerved by Veronica's extreme reaction, as Harry watched them all with a puzzled look on his face.

"May I ask what we're all talking about? From what I can gather, the girls have been invited to a meeting sponsored by the Grand Wizard of the Ku Klux Klan, and Veronica wishes to decline."

"Exactly," Veronica said, pacing around the room and fuming, as Ginny looked at her mother in horror.

"Do you mean we can't do it?" Ginny asked with a look of panic. "Mom, don't let her spoil it . . . *everyone* is doing it. Two of the girls already got dresses at Saks this weekend!" Ginny was obviously terrified of getting a late start.

"Relax, both of you," Olympia said, setting dinner down on the table, handing Virginia a tissue and trying to exude a sense of calm she didn't feel. She hadn't expected either girl's reaction to be quite so extreme. "We'll talk about it. This isn't a meeting of the Ku Klux Klan, for God's sake, Veronica. It's a coming-out party. I did it, your grandmothers did it, your great-grandmothers did it. And you'll have fun doing it with your sister."

"I would rather *die*!" Veronica shouted at her.

"Mom, I *want* to do it!" Ginny said, and cried harder, jumping up from the table, too.

"You would!" Veronica shouted at her sister, with tears bulging in her eyes, too. "It's the dumbest idea I've ever heard. It's insulting. It makes us look like snobby racist morons! I'd rather be in a peace march, or digging ditches in Appalachia or Nicaragua, or anywhere, than in a stupid white dress, showing off to a lot of dumb, snobby peo-

ple who have totally sick political ideas! Mom," she said, turning to her mother with a steely look in her eyes, "I *won't* do it! I don't care what you do to me. I *won't.*" And then she turned toward her sister with a look of utterly outraged disgust. "And if you want to, frankly, I think you're *sick*!" With that, she stormed out of the kitchen, and a few seconds later, they heard her slam the door to her room, as Ginny stood in the middle of the room and sobbed.

"She always does that! You can't let her do this, Mom! She ruins *everything*!"

"She hasn't ruined everything. You're both overreacting. Why don't we let everyone cool off for a day or two, and talk about it again. She'll calm down. Just leave her alone."

"She *won't* calm down," Ginny said with a look of anguish. "She's a *Communist* and I hate her!" And with that, Ginny ran out of the room in tears. A moment later they heard the door of her room slam, too, as Harry looked across the table at his wife in amazement and total consternation.

"May I ask what's going on? What are The Arches, for God's sake, and what got into the girls?" Two of their children appeared to have gone insane. Max dug into his baked potato, and calmly shook his head.

"Mom wants them to find husbands," Max said simply, "and I don't think they want to. Maybe Ginny does, because she likes boys more than Ver does. It sounds to me like Ver doesn't want to get married. Right, Mom?"

"No . . . yes . . . no, of course not." Olympia looked flustered as she sat down and looked at both of them. "It used to be about finding husbands; it isn't anymore," she explained to Max again, and then looked at Harry, brushing a lock of hair out of her eyes. The kitchen suddenly seemed far too warm. The evening had gotten far more heated than she expected. She was visibly upset about both girls. She turned to Harry, and tried to appear calmer than she felt. "The girls have been invited to come out at The Arches. The invitation came on Friday. I thought it would be fun for them. I came out at The Arches, and honestly, Harry, it's no big deal."

"I'm sorry. I'm in the dark here. The only arches I know about are the ones at McDonald's. Why are we arguing about them coming out of McDonald's? Something tells me I'm missing some major piece of information here."

"The Arches is a debutante cotillion. It's the oldest and most respected one in the city. In serious social circles, it's a big deal. It was a much bigger deal when I was their age. My mother came out there, and both my grandmothers, and my great-grandmothers. Nowadays, it's just a nice party, and something of an archaic tradition. It's harmless. They wear pretty dresses and waltz with their fathers. Veronica is trying to turn this into a political event. It isn't. It's just a party, for God's sake, and apparently Ginny wants to do it."

"Can anyone sign up for this event?" Harry inquired with a cautious look.

"No, you have to be invited. The girls were, because they're a legacy," she said simply.

"Does it exclude people of other races and religions?" Harry then asked her pointedly. This time Olympia hesitated slightly before she answered, as Max managed to eat his baked potato and watch them with interest at the same time. He was dripping butter all over his shirt with total unconcern.

"Probably. It used to. I don't know what their policies are these days."

"Judging by Veronica's reaction, she seems to know more than you do. If what she says is true, and black, Asian, and Hispanic girls can't do it, then I agree with her. And I assume Jewish girls would be on their hit list, too."

"Oh for God's sake, Harry. Yes, it's a fancy social thing. People have been doing it for years. It's old-fashioned, it's traditional, it's Waspy, so is the Social Register, so are clubs, for heaven's sake. What about clubs that don't admit women?"

"I don't belong to a single one of them," he said succinctly. "I'm a judge on the court of appeals, I can't afford to ally myself with any discriminatory organization, and apparently this one is. You know how I feel about things like that. Do you think they would invite our daughter, if we had one, if they knew you are now Jewish?" It was an interesting question, but the girls were not Jewish, and they were descended from two powerful, well-known, aristocratic WASP families. And she and Harry didn't have a daughter. The question was moot for them. She knew without a doubt that Chauncey expected his daughters to come out. He would have been horrified if they didn't. And even though she was far more liberal than her ex-husband or his wife, she still felt it was a harmless tradition. She thought Harry was overreacting, and so were the girls.

"I understand about the discriminatory aspect. This isn't intended to hurt people, just to give some girls a night of fun. It's like being Cinderella. They wear a pretty white dress, and at midnight it's over. Is that so terrible, so wrong? Why is that such a big deal?"

"Because it excludes people. Nazi Germany was founded on principles just like these. This is an Aryan elitist party, the girls being presented, if that's what you call it, are Aryans presumably. Maybe they have a token Jew or two, but the whole concept is wrong, the principles are wrong. Jews have been discriminated against for thousands of years. I don't support upholding that tradition. In order to be politically correct in today's world, everyone should be able to sign up if they want to do it."

"If that were true, clubs wouldn't exist. Private schools wouldn't exist. Okay, call it a club for WASPs, where their daughters make their debut. I just don't see why this has to be a political issue. Why can't this just be a fun night for the girls and let it go at that?"

"My mother is a Holocaust survivor," he said ominously. "You know that. And so was my father. Their entire families were wiped out by people who hated Jews. The people who run this party are racists, from what I can gather. That runs counter to everything I stand for and believe in. I want nothing to do with an event like this." He spoke to her as though she had just painted a swastika on their kitchen wall. He almost recoiled as he spoke to her, and their son watched, looking suddenly upset.

"Harry, please, don't make a big deal out of this. It's a coming-out party, that's all it is."

"Veronica is right," he said quietly, and then stood up. He hadn't touched a mouthful of his dinner. Olympia hadn't cut Max's meat, so he was working on his second baked potato. He was hungry. And the grown-ups were confusing. "I don't think the girls should participate in this party," Harry said firmly, "whether you did it or not.

I'm casting my vote with Veronica. And whatever you decide to do about it, don't for a single second expect me to attend." With that, he threw his napkin on the table and walked out of the room, while Max stared after his father, and then looked at his mother with worried eyes.

"Sounds like the party is a bad idea," Max said sadly. "Everybody got really mad."

"Yes, they did," Olympia said with a sigh, sitting back in her chair and looking at him. "It's just a party, Max, that's all it is." He was the only one left to explain it to, and he was only five years old.

"Are they going to do bad things to Jews there?" he asked, looking worried. He knew from his grandmother that people called Nazis had done terrible things, although he did not know the details. He knew they had done them to Jews, and he knew that he and his parents were Jewish, as were his grandmother and many of his friends at school.

"Of course they're not going to do bad things to Jews there," Olympia said, looking horrified. "Daddy was just upset. No one is going to do anything to Jews."

"That's good," Max said, looking slightly

reassured. "I guess they're not going to go to the party, though, huh? I think Ginny wanted a new dress."

"Yes, she did. I don't know if they'll do it or not, but I think they should."

"Even if you can't get husbands for them?" Max asked with interest.

"Even if we can't get husbands for them," Olympia said, smiling ruefully. "We don't want husbands for them, sweetheart. All we want are a couple of white dresses, and some boys to dance with them."

"I don't think Dad will go," Max said, shaking his head, as his mother cut his meat. They were the only two at the table, and Olympia had no desire to eat. She knew the girls' father would have a fit if they didn't make their debut. Politically, he was at the opposite end of the spectrum from Harry. Her old life and her new, as typified by both husbands, had absolutely nothing in common. She was the bridge between the two.

"I hope Daddy will go," Olympia said quietly to her son. "It's a fun thing to do."

"It doesn't sound like fun to me," Max said, shaking his head solemnly. "I don't think Ginny and Ver should come out," he said, looking up at his mother with wide eyes. "I think they better stay in." Given everyone's reactions that night, it was beginning to sound like it to her, too.

Chapter 2

Olympia called her ex-husband from the office the next day, and explained the situation to him. She told him simply that Virginia wanted to come out, Veronica had objected to it, and she said somewhat unhappily that she thought there was a possibility that Veronica would not give in. There had been another explosion over it at breakfast that morning, before they left for school. Veronica was threatening to move in with her stepgrandmother if her mother didn't agree to let her off the hook, and Harry had seconded the idea. He added fuel to the fire by saying that he didn't think either girl should come out, and Ginny had left for school in tears, after saying she hated him. Overnight the family had erupted in civil war. Virginia had called her brother the night before, and although he sympathized with Veronica's objections to the event, he sided with Virginia and Olympia, and said he thought both girls should come out. All their cousins in Newport had, and he knew, as Olympia did, that their father would be upset if they didn't. Harry would be upset if they did. One way or the other, everyone was going to be unhappy about something. Olympia and Harry hadn't even been speaking to each other when they both left for work, which was a rare occurrence for them. They hardly ever fought. But this time, the battle lines had been drawn.

Predictably, as always, Chauncey did not make things better, but worse.

"What kind of rabble-rousing left-wing household are you running there, Olympia, if Veronica thinks that making her debut is a persecution of the Great Unwashed? You all sound like a bunch of Commies to me." It was just the kind of thing Olympia expected him to say.

"Oh for God's sake, Chauncey, they're kids. They get emotional. Veronica has always had extreme political ideas; she's the champion of the underdog. She thinks she's a combination of Mother Teresa and Che Guevara. She'll outgrow it. This is her way of expressing herself. Seven months from now, I think she'll calm down and do it, if we don't make too big a deal of it now. If we do, she'll dig her heels in. So let's be reasonable, please." Someone had to be. And apparently Chauncey wasn't going to be either, which was no surprise to her.

"Well, let me tell you where I stand on this, Olympia," he said, sounding incredibly arrogant and haughty, which was typical of him. "I'm not going to tolerate having a revolutionary as a daughter, and I think that should be nipped in the bud right now. You should have done it years ago, if that's the direction she was heading in. I'm not going to tolerate this Communist crap from any of you, if you understand what I mean. If she decides that it is too politically right-wing to make her debut at The Arches, then I'm not going to pay her tuition at Brown next year. She can go and dig ditches in Nicaragua or El Salvador, or wherever she thinks she should be doing it, and see how she likes the life of a political radical. And if she's not careful, she'll wind up in jail."

"She's not going to jail, Chauncey,"

Olympia said, sounding exasperated. He was the other end of the spectrum, and possibly why Veronica was so extreme in reaction to him. There was no one on the planet more snobbish than Chauncey and his wife. They thought the entire world had polo ponies, or should, and that no one existed on earth except people listed in the Social Register. She didn't like his point of view, either. If she had to choose one ideology, she liked Harry's better, but he was being silly too. "She has a strong social conscience. We just have to let her calm down, and hopefully when she does, she'll see that no one is being hurt by this. It's just a fun evening, and something nice for them to do. Don't get in an argument with her, and if you threaten her about tuition, she's liable to do something ridiculous and decide not to go to school."

"This is what you get for marrying a radical Jew." His words rang out like shots, as she sat immobilized in her seat. She couldn't believe he had the nerve to say something like that. She wanted to strangle him.

"What did you just say?" she said in an icy tone.

"You heard what I said," he fired back at her in clipped, aristocratic tones. He sounded so snobby sometimes that he sounded like a 1930s movie. No one spoke that way anymore, at any level of society, only Chauncey and Felicia did, and a handful of snobs like them.

"Don't you *ever* say something like that to me again. You're not fit to wipe his feet. It's no wonder Veronica is off the deep end over this, with an example like you. My God, have you ever bothered to notice that there's a whole world of people out there, not just idiots like you, with polo ponies?" He hadn't had a real job in twenty years. First he had lived off his grandmother, then his inheritance, and she suspected they lived off Felicia's trust funds, too. They were a worthless lot who had never done anything for the human race and never would. Maybe Veronica was trying to atone for their sins of indifference to the rest of the human race.

"You lost your mind when you converted, Olympia. I've never understood how you could do that. You're a Crawford, for chrissake."

"No, I'm a Rubenstein," she said clearly. "I

love my husband. My converting was important to him. And it's none of your business. My religion is my business, not yours." She was furious with him. He was precisely the kind of racist that Harry was objecting to when he said he wouldn't go.

"You betrayed your entire heritage just to please a man who's left of Lenin." Chauncey stood his ground.

"You don't know what you're talking about. What we're discussing here is a party we want our daughters to attend, not your politics or mine. Leave Lenin to me. The problem is Veronica, not Harry."

"They sound like one and the same to me." In fact, at the moment they were, but she wasn't about to admit that to him. First she had to get Veronica calmed down, then she could work on Harry. He was a reasonable man, and she knew that eventually he'd come around. Chauncey was another story, and if there was an opportunity to be irritating, ignorant, and inflammatory, he would seize it every time. And Felicia was even dumber than he. Olympia could no longer even remotely imagine how she had ever married him, even at twenty-two. At forty-four, she would rather have cut her head off than be married to him for ten minutes. Just talking to him drove her insane.

"I don't want you threatening Veronica about her tuition. If you do that, she'll do something even more stupid. Let's keep this about the party, and not about tuition or school. You can't do that to the girls. I can take you to court over it if I have to." He had an obligation to pay the girls' tuition, although she knew he was foolish enough not to pay it just to prove a point, despite the consequences to him.

"Go ahead, take me to court, Olympia. I don't give a damn if you do. If you don't give Veronica my message, I will. In fact, just to make sure she doesn't do something stupid, you can tell her I won't pay tuition for either of them, unless they both come out next Christmas. Veronica won't want to screw it up for Ginny, and if Veronica doesn't agree to come out, she will. I don't care if you put me in jail. I'm not paying a red cent for either of them, unless they both make their debut. Put Veronica in handcuffs, or sedate her if you have to, but she *will* come out at The Arches!" He was every bit as stubborn as his daughter, and more so. He was turning this into a major war for all of them. Everyone was out of control, and all over a debut.

"That's not fair to do to Virginia. That's blackmail, Chauncey. The poor thing is already in a total state over Veronica's position. Ginny wants to come out, it's not her fault her sister is being unreasonable. Don't you be unreasonable, too."

"I'm taking Virginia as a hostage, to bring Veronica to her senses." And he was taking her hostage, too. She had no desire to take legal action against him over tuition. The kids would hate her for it, Veronica would be even more outraged, and she knew even Charlie would be upset. It was utterly absurd and not an empty threat from him. She knew Chauncey was foolish enough to do it and follow through.

"Oh for God's sake, Chauncey, that's a rotten thing to do. It's just a party, it's not worth two families warring over it, and not paying the girls' college tuition." Not to mention the fact that paying both tuitions in full, in addition to her share of Charlie's, would take a big bite out of her, which would infuriate Harry further. They could afford it, but Chauncey should pay for his own kids. And punishing Ginny for Veronica's stance seemed disgusting to her. But that was Chauncey, always manipulative to the nth degree. She hated him for it, and had for years. He was always putting the squeeze on her for something, and now he was doing it again, over a debutante party. It was beginning to sound crazy to her, too.

"I'm not going to have a daughter who won't come out. For heaven's sake, Olympia, think of the embarrassment that will cause."

"I can think of worse things," Olympia said glumly. But Chauncey couldn't, obviously. Not being a debutante was worse than death to him. Olympia wanted them to have fun, even if it seemed silly, but she wasn't willing to threaten their lives over it. If Veronica truly refused to do it, she wasn't going to force her, and Virginia could still come out, with or without her twin. Chauncey's ploy of holding her hostage was just too extreme, and too unfair, to all of them, her too.

"I can't think of anything more humiliating, and I'm not going to be pushed around by her. You can tell her I said so, Olympia."

"Why don't you tell her yourself?" Olympia said, tired of being in the middle. It was just going to make Veronica madder at her. If he wanted to threaten her to that degree, let him do it himself.

"I will," he said, sounding furious. "I don't know how you've brought up these girls. At least Ginny has some sense."

"I think we need to let this cool down," Olympia said sensibly. "We can deal with it in September, or later. I'll sign both girls up, and send in the check." It was a negligible amount anyway. It wasn't about ability to pay, it was about the color of the blood in your veins. Anything other than blue was not acceptable. "Veronica doesn't even need to know she's been signed up. We can tell her that we'll decide in the fall, and give it a rest over the summer."

"I don't want there to be any doubt in her mind that she's coming out next winter. I want to make that clear to her."

"I'm sure you will," her mother said, imagining the explosion that would cause. Veronica was going to turn this into a cause célèbre, with her father's provocation and help. He was an idiot about handling people, and had never dealt with either of the girls well, nor her. He had the subtlety of a Mack truck, and values that made even Olympia want to become a "Communist," as he referred to it. Anything, as long as it was as far from him as one could get. "If they need photographs of the girls, I can send them two of Virginia." With identical twins, they would never know the difference, fortunately. "Ginny and I can buy her a dress. Why don't you just let it be, Chauncey. I'll take care of it on my end."

"Make sure you do. If she doesn't capitulate, I'll step in."

"Thanks for your help," she said sarcastically, and it went right over his head.

"Do you want Felicia to talk to her?" Olympia nearly groaned at the suggestion. Felicia was not known for her tact, nor her popularity with either girl. They tolerated her for their father's sake, but thought her irritating and stupid. Olympia agreed.

"I'll deal with it myself." She managed to get off the phone with him before she lost her temper, which was a minor miracle. Everything about Chauncey Walker made her want to strangle him. She was still furious about their conversation, when her mother-in-law called her that afternoon. Olympia was up to her ears in work, preparing a case for litigation, when her secretary told her that Mrs. Rubinstein was on the phone. Olympia had no idea what it was about. She just hoped it wasn't the ball. Harry whining to his mother was unlike him, but anything seemed possible now. The whole family was up in arms, from Newport to New York.

"Hi, Frieda," Olympia said, sounding tired. She was stressed about the family issues, and had had a long day at work. "Everything all right?"

"You tell me. Veronica called and said she was mad at you, and wants to spend the night." Olympia pursed her lips. She didn't like the idea of Veronica trying to run away from irritants at home, although she valued the close relationship both girls had with Harry's mother. She was a kind, warm, wise woman with a heart of gold, and loved Olympia's children like her own. "I wanted to check what you want me to do."

"I appreciate that. Actually, I think I'd like her to stick around for a few days and work it out, or at least let things calm down. Maybe she could stay with you on the weekend, with Max, if you want him, too."

"That's fine. You know I love having them stay with me. Do you want to send Ginny, too?"

"The girls are at odds with each other, actually," Olympia said with a sigh.

"What about?"

"It's too stupid to talk about, and it's hard to explain." Frieda didn't tell her daughter-in-law that Harry already had.

He had come to lunch, which was unusual, and had vented to her. Her perspective on it had been markedly different from his, and she hadn't hesitated to say so. She told him he was making far too much of it, and said the party sounded like fun to her. She didn't feel singled out for discrimination or persecution. And when he told her sarcastically it was a racist event, she scolded him for being ridiculous and overreacting. It was no different than any club. And this one was a club for young Protestant girls. She pointed out to him that there were no Irish Catholic women in her Hadassah chapter either, and no one was going nuts over them, or boycotting them. All clubs had the right to let in who they wanted, and she thought this would be a wonderful experience for the girls. She thought Veronica should do it, and intended to tell her so, if she had the chance. Harry told her she was far too liberal for his taste, and left her apartment in a huff after lunch. He was still upset when he went back to his office. Olympia hadn't heard from him all day. "I'm sorry Veronica bothered you with this," Olympia apologized. "It's a tempest in a teapot, but for the moment, everyone's getting burned, and very steamed up."

"How can I help?" Frieda said practically. She was a wonderful, intelligent woman, with a youthful outlook for her age, and an incredibly forgiving nature, given the childhood experiences she'd had. She rarely if ever talked about it, but Olympia knew from Harry how terrifying and devastating it was for her, losing her entire family, and living through the torture in the camps. She had had nightmares for years, and had very wisely undergone therapy. Her attitude was extraordinary, and Olympia had nothing but the profoundest affection and respect for her. She felt blessed to be related to her.

"I don't think you can help, Frieda. They'll all settle down. It's a long, silly story. The girls were invited to make their debut at the ball where I came out years ago. It's an archaic tradition, but a nice one for the girls who want to participate. There are fools like Chauncey who try to make it a prerequisite for real life, which it isn't. It's just a very pretty, superficial, but lovely Cinderella night. As far as I can see, it doesn't do anyone any harm. I guess it's elitist, but Harry thinks it's a neo-Nazi event. Veronica thinks I'm a fascist. Chauncey thinks we're Communists, and says he won't pay the girls' college tuition if they don't both come out, which is unfair. Veronica hasn't heard that piece of it yet, but as of this morning, she was refusing to do it, and threatening to move in with you, since my values are so terrible. And Ginny is desperate to do it. Harry says he won't come, and acts like he's going to divorce me. Charlie is mad at Veronica. The girls are at each other's throats, and everyone hates me. The only sane one left in the family is Max, who says this coming-out thing is such a mess that the girls better stay in." They both laughed at Max's sensible advice. "I don't know what to do. It's not worth all this turmoil, but out of pure nostalgia and a sense of tradition, I'd love them to do it. I never thought it would turn out to be such a big deal to everyone. I'm beginning to feel like a monster for asking them to do it. And Harry is furious with me." She sounded profoundly unhappy as she explained it all to Frieda.

"Tell them all to take a hike," the older woman said sanely. "Go shopping for a dress with Ginny, and buy one for Veronica. Tell my son to get over himself. The Nazis are setting fire to synagogues in Germany, they don't have time for white-tie events, or even black-tie ones." She had said exactly that to him herself. "Don't pay any attention to them. Veronica needs to let off steam. She'll do it in the end. What are you going to wear?" Frieda asked with a tone of interest, and Olympia laughed. It was the most sensible question she could have asked.

"A straitjacket if they don't all calm down." And then she thought of something, and wondered how her mother-in-law would react, given what Harry had said. "Frieda, would you like to come?"

"Are you serious?" She sounded stunned. From what Harry had said, she had assumed that wouldn't be possible, if the event was in fact anti-Semitic, and she would never have asked to come, nor expected it. Even operating under that assumption, she still thought the twins should come out, whether or not she was there.

She was extremely generous about never forcing herself on her daughter-in-law, her son, or their children. She was incredibly discreet, and had been wonderful to Olympia from the first, unlike her first mother-in-law, who had been a beast, and the biggest snob on earth, just like her son. The apple hadn't fallen far from the tree, in either case.

"Of course I'm serious," Olympia reassured her, grateful for her support.

"I thought Jews and blacks weren't allowed," she said cautiously. It was what Harry had said over lunch, and one of the reasons why he was so upset.

"They didn't print it on the invitation, for heaven's sake," although admittedly, in the old days, there had been unspoken rules of exclusion. But she assumed all that had changed. She hadn't been to a deb ball in years. The Arches was the most distinguished debutante cotillion of all, and the most exclusive by far. But she wouldn't have thought of not inviting Frieda to join them at the event, no matter what anyone thought or what the current standards were. "Who cares what they think? You're our family, and the girls would be devastated if you weren't there. So would I."

"Oh my God . . . I never thought . . . I never imagined . . . Harry will be furious . . . but I'd love to come. What'll I wear?"

Olympia laughed, relieved. Her mother-in-law sounded thrilled.

"We'll find something. You and I can go shopping in the fall. We'll buy something very grand." Olympia suddenly realized it was a big deal to her mother-in-law, as much as it was to Ginny, and to Harry in the opposite sense. It represented everything she had been excluded from and cheated of as a young girl, and was a form of victory and validation for her. There had been no balls or parties in her youth. There had been poverty and hard work in sweatshops. Knowing that her daughter-in-law wanted her at an event like that meant the world to her, and Olympia wouldn't have deprived her of it for anything on earth. Olympia could hear in Frieda's voice how much it meant to her.

"I have to find something with long sleeves," she said softly, and Olympia understood. She wanted to cover her tattoo, as she always did.

"We'll find the perfect dress. I promise," Olympia said gently.

"Good. I'll work on Veronica this weekend. She shouldn't spoil it for her sister. Cesar Chavez will never know she went, and it'll be more fun for both of them if they both go. And tell my son not to be such a pain in the neck. He just doesn't want to wear a tux. And if he won't go, we'll have a good time without him. December is a long way off, they'll all calm down by then. Don't let them upset you," Frieda said in a loving tone, which was typical of all of Olympia's dealings with her in the thirteen years of her marriage to Harry. Olympia had won her mother-in-law's love and loyalty forever when she converted to Judaism. She was a terrific girl, and Frieda said she saw nothing wrong with the girls making their debut at an exclusive WASP social event. In fact, she was thrilled to go herself. "I'll put it on my calendar that we'll shop in September, as soon as the fall dresses come in. I'm thinking maybe black velvet. How does that sound to you?"

"It sounds like you're the most wonderful woman I know," Olympia said with tears in her eyes. "I'm lucky to know you."

"Just forget about it. Everything will be fine. Harry will get over it. He's just being stupid and overreacting." They all were. "He should relax his principles for one night, enjoy it and eat his dinner, and not give you such a hard time."

Olympia felt better as soon as they hung up. But, in spite of her mother-in-law's comforting assurances, she still looked tired and stressed. It was nearly five o'clock, and she wanted to get home to Max. One of her partners walked into her office five minutes later, and saw the look on Olympia's face.

"You look like you've had a fun day," Margaret Washington said with a tired smile. She'd had a tough day herself, working on an appeal of a class action suit they had brought against a string of factories that were dumping toxic waste, and lost. She was one of the firm's best lawyers. She went to Harvard as an undergraduate, and then on to Yale Law School. She happened to be African American and Olympia wasn't anxious to explain her problems to her, but after circling the subject cautiously for five minutes, she finally spelled it out to her. Margaret had exactly the same reaction Olympia's mother-in-law had had. "Oh for chrissake, we poison the environment, we sell cigarettes and alcohol, half the nation's youth is hooked on drugs they can buy on street corners, not to mention guns, we have one of the highest suicide rates in the world among youth under the age of twenty-five, we get into wars that are none of our goddamn business at every opportunity, Social Security is bankrupt or damn near it, the nation is crippled by debt. Our politicians are crooked for the most part, our educational system is falling apart, and you're supposed to feel guilty about your kids playing Cinderella for one night at some fancy Waspy ball? Give me a break. I've got news for you, there are no whites at my mother's bingo club in Harlem either, and she doesn't feel guilty for a goddamn minute. Harry knows better—why don't you tell him to go picket someone? This isn't a Nazi youth movement, it's a bunch of silly girls in pretty white dresses. Hell, if I were in your shoes, and I had a kid, I'd want her to do it, too. And I wouldn't feel guilty about it, either. Tell everyone to relax. It doesn't bother me, and I boycotted just about everything on the planet all through college and law school. This one wouldn't even have raised my eyebrows."

"That's what my mother-in-law said. Harry said it was a disrespect to every member of his family who died in the Holocaust. He made me feel like Eva Braun."

"Your mother-in-law sounds a lot more sensible. What else did she say?" Margaret asked with interest. She was a spectacular-looking woman, a few years younger than Olympia, and she had modeled in college. She had been in *Harper's Bazaar* and *Vogue* in order to supplement her scholarship at Harvard.

"She wanted to know what I thought of black velvet, and how soon we could shop for her dress."

"Precisely. My sentiments exactly. Fuck all of them, Ollie. Tell your revolutionary kid to shape up, and your husband to give it up. This isn't on the ACLU's radar screen, it doesn't need to be on his either. And your ex-husband sounds like a real jerk."

"He is. If he gets a chance, he'll stir the pot. He'd rather have a kid on life support than one not making her debut. I just want them to have fun, and do the same thing I did. In my day, it wasn't a big deal, it was just something you did. I did it in the seventies, in the sixties everyone refused to, in the forties and fifties you had to, to find a husband. It isn't about that anymore, it's about wearing a dress and going to a party. That's all it is. A one-night stand for tradition and the family album. Not a travesty of social values."

"Believe me, I never lost a night's sleep over it when I was a kid, and I knew girls at Harvard who did it in New York and Boston. In fact, one of them invited me to go, but I was modeling in Chicago that weekend to pay for school."

"I hope you come," Olympia said generously, and Margaret grinned.

"I'd love to." It never even remotely occurred to Olympia that Margaret being there would cause a stir, nor did she care. So far, she had invited a Jewish woman as her guest, and an African American, and she was Jewish now herself. And if the committee didn't like it for some reason, though she doubted it, she didn't give a damn.

"I just hope Harry comes, too," she said, looking sad. She hated fighting with him.

"If he doesn't, it's his loss, and he'll look stupid. Give him time to come down off his high horse. It should tell him something that his mother approves and thinks the girls should do it."

"Yeah," Olympia said with a sigh. "Now all I have to do is convince the girls. Or Veronica at least. If not, she and Harry can picket the event. Maybe they can carry signs objecting to the women wearing fur."

They both laughed, and half an hour later Olympia went home. The atmosphere at home was strained that night. None of them said a word at dinner, but at least this time everyone sat down and ate. By the time they went to bed that night, Harry had unbent a little. She didn't discuss the deb ball with him, nor with Veronica. She didn't touch the subject with either of them, until Veronica went berserk three days later when she got a letter from her father.

He had written her the threat not to pay her or Ginny's college tuition if both girls didn't come out, and she ranted and raved at how disgusting he was, how manipulative, and how horrible to hold her hostage and blackmail her. Olympia didn't comment on his threat, but she noticed that the girls made peace with each other after that. Veronica didn't say that she would come out, but she no longer said she wouldn't, either. She didn't want her actions to hurt her sister, or to force her mother to pay for their entire tuition. She was furious with her father now, and commented liberally on what shit values he had, what a bastard he was, and how stupid the whole thing was.

Olympia sent her check in to The Arches for both of them, and assured them that both girls were thrilled to attend the ball. She said nothing more about it to Harry, and figured they had plenty of time to work it out before December. His only comment to her was late one night after Charlie came home from Dartmouth for the weekend and mentioned it. Harry said only three words to both of them, which said it all.

"I'm not going," he growled, and then left the room, leaving Olympia to discuss it with her elder son.

"That's fine," Olympia said quietly, remembering what his mother had said, and Margaret Washington. She had seven months to change his mind.

Charlie agreed to be Ginny's escort for the ball, although she had recently met a boy she liked. She had taken her mother's advice about not inviting a romantic interest to be her escort for the ball. A lot could change in seven months. Olympia was counting on it. She still needed to turn Harry and Veronica around. For the moment at least, everyone seemed to have calmed down.

Chapter 3

When Charlie came home from Dartmouth for the summer, he seemed quiet to his mother. He had done well in school, was playing varsity tennis, had played ice hockey all winter, and was starting to take up golf. He saw all his friends, hung out with his sisters, and went on a date with one of Veronica's friends. He took Max out to throw a ball in Central Park, and took him to a beach on Long Island in June. But no matter how busy he was, Olympia was worried about him. He seemed quieter than usual to her, distant, and out of sorts. He was leaving soon for his job at the camp in Colorado, and claimed he was looking forward to it. Olympia couldn't put her finger on it, but he seemed sad to her, and uncomfortable in his own skin.

She mentioned it to Harry after they played tennis one Saturday morning, while Charlie babysat for Max. She and Harry loved playing tennis and squash with each other. It gave them time alone and relaxed them both. They cherished the time they managed to spend alone, which was infrequent, as they spent most of their evenings and weekend time with Max. With Charlie home, they had a built-in babysitter. He was always quick to volunteer to take care of Max for them.

"I haven't noticed anything," Harry said, wiping his face with a towel, after the game. He had beaten her, but barely. They had both played a good game, and were in great shape. She had just shared her concerns about Charlie with him, and he was surprised to hear that Olympia thought Charlie was out of sorts. "He seems fine to me."

"He doesn't to me. He hasn't said anything, but whenever he doesn't know I'm watching him, he looks depressed, or pensive, or just sad somehow. Or worried. I don't know what it is. Maybe he's unhappy at school."

"You worry too much, Ollie," he said, smiling at her, and then he leaned over and kissed her. "That was a good game. I had fun."

"Yeah." She grinned at him as he put an arm around her. "Because you won. You always say it was a good game when you win."

"You beat me the last time we played squash."

"Only because you pulled a hamstring. Without that, you always beat me. You play squash better than I do." But she often beat him at tennis. It didn't really matter to her who won, she just liked being with him, even after all these years.

"You're a better lawyer than I was," Harry said, and she looked startled. He had never said that to her before.

"No, I'm not. Don't be silly. You were a fantastic lawyer. What do you mean? You're just trying to make me feel better because you beat me at tennis."

"No, I'm not. You are a better lawyer than I am, Ollie. I knew it even when you were a law student. You have a solid, powerful, meticulous way of doing what you do, and at the same time you manage to be creative about it. Some of what you do is absolutely brilliant. I admire your work a lot. I was always very methodical about my cases when I was practicing. But I never had the kind of creativity you do. Some of it is truly inspired."

"Wow! Do you mean that?" She looked at him with gratitude and pleasure. It was the nicest compliment he had ever paid her about her work.

"Yes, I do. If I needed legal advice, I'd come to you in a hot minute. I'm not sure I'd want you as my tennis teacher. But as my lawyer, anytime." She shoved him gently then, and he kissed her. She always had a good time with him. And she was pleased to see that he'd relaxed finally, after their battles about the ball. He still said he wasn't coming, but she hadn't mentioned it to him in a while. She wanted to let the subject cool off before she tried again.

They talked about Charlie again as they walked home. "I just have the feeling something is bothering him, but he doesn't seem to want to talk."

"If you're right, he'll talk to you eventually," Harry reassured her. "He always does." He knew how close Olympia was to her older son, just as she was to the twins, and to Max. She was a terrific mother, and a wonderful wife. There was so much he admired about her and always had. Just as she loved and respected him. And he knew she had great instincts for her kids. If she thought something was upsetting Charlie, maybe she was right, although she felt more relaxed about it after discussing it with Harry. "Maybe he got his heart broken over some girl." They both wondered if it was that. Charlie hadn't had a serious romance in a while. He went out a lot, and played the field. He hadn't had a serious girl in his life in nearly two years.

"I don't think it's that. I think he'd tell me if it was about a girl. It seems deeper than that to me. He just looks sad."

"Working at the camp in Colorado will do him good," Harry said as they reached their front door. They could hear both boys rough-housing as soon as they walked in. Charlie was playing cowboys and Indians with Max, and you could hear their bloodcurdling war whoops halfway down the block. Charlie had used toothpaste and her lipstick as war paint on his face, and the minute their mother saw them, she laughed.

Max was running around the house, brandishing a toy gun at his older brother, wearing a cowboy hat and his underpants. Harry joined the fun, while Olympia went to make them all lunch. It had been a lovely morning.

But she grew more concerned again a few days later, when she got a bill from Dartmouth for counseling services. She mentioned it to Charlie discreetly, and he insisted he was fine. He told her a friend of his had committed suicide during second semester and it had upset him terribly at the time, but he was feeling better now. Hearing about it worried her, she didn't want him getting the same idea, and she remembered reading about kids who showed no sign of stress, and then committed suicide without warning. When she told Harry about it, he told her she was being neurotic, and reminded her that the fact that he had gotten counseling was a good sign. It was usually kids who didn't get therapy or counseling who went off the deep end. Charlie seemed fine to him. They played golf together over several weekends, and Charlie came down to have lunch at his office. He said he was thinking of going to divinity school after he graduated, and the ministry appealed to him. Harry was impressed by what he said, and the insights he had about people and delicate situations. Charlie broached the deb ball with him once or twice, and Harry refused to discuss it with him. He said that he disapproved of an event that excluded anyone, tacitly or otherwise, and he had taken a stand.

So had Veronica, but her position seemed to be softening by the time the girls left for Europe in July with their friends. Ginny had ordered a dress by then, a beautiful white taffeta strapless ballgown with tiny pearls sewn in a flower pattern in a wide border along the hem. It looked like a wedding gown, and Ginny was thrilled with it. And without saying anything to Veronica, Ginny and her mother had chosen a narrow white satin column with a diagonal band across one shoulder that looked like something Veronica would wear. It was sexy, sleek, and backless and would show off her slim figure. Ginny preferred her big ballgown. Both dresses were exquisite, and although the girls were identical, the dresses would set off the differences between them, and underline their contrasting styles. Olympia had hidden the satin dress in her closet and sworn Virginia to secrecy that they had shopped for it at all. And before they left for Europe, Ginny had posed in both dresses for the ball program. They didn't need to discuss it with Veronica at all. There were photographs of both girls now, or seemed to be. If she had a fit again later, they'd deal with it. For now, all was calm.

The girls were in good spirits when they left for Europe, and on good terms with each other. Charlie left for Colorado two days later, and Olympia and Harry left for their trip to France with Max. They had a wonderful time in Paris, went to every monument and museum, and took Max to the Jardin du Luxembourg. He had a ball playing with French children, and enjoyed all the rides. At night, they took Max out to bistros with them. He ate pizza, and steak with *pommes frites.* They went to Berthillon on the Île St. Louis for ice cream, and Max loved the crêpes they bought in the street in St. Germain. And they took him to the top of the Eiffel Tower. They had a wonderful trip, and in spite of Max sleeping in the adjoining room from them, Harry and Olympia had a romantic time. They stayed at a small hotel Harry knew on the Left Bank. And all three of them were sorry to leave Paris. On their last night, they had taken a long slow ride on a Bâteau Mouche on the Seine, admiring the lights of Paris and the beautiful buildings and monuments as they glided by.

After that, they went to the Riviera. They spent a few days in St. Tropez, a night in Monte Carlo, and a few days in Cannes. Max played on the beach, and started picking up a few words of French from a group of children his own age. At the end of a week, all three of them were rested, happy, and tanned. They had spent the whole week eating bouillabaisse, lobster, and fish. Max sent Charlie a T-shirt from St. Tropez, and Charlie sent them a steady stream of funny postcards, reporting on his adventures in camp. He seemed to be having a great time.

They were once again sad to leave, when Olympia, Harry, and Max flew from Nice to Venice to meet the girls. And all five of them had a terrific time in Venice. They visited every church and monument. Max fed the pigeons in the Piazza San Marco, and they all took a gondola ride under the Bridge of Sighs. Harry kissed Olympia as they passed under it, which the gondolier said meant they would belong to each other forever. As they kissed, Max scrunched his face up and the twins smiled at them and laughed at Max.

Their subsequent trip through northern Italy and into Switzerland was an unforgettable family time. They stayed at a beautiful hotel on Lake Geneva, traveled through the Alps, and wound up in London for the last few days. Max said he had loved all of it, and they all admitted that they were sad the twins were leaving for college. The house was going to be deadly quiet without them. On the flight back to New York, Olympia was quiet, wishing the girls wouldn't be leaving home so soon. The trip to Europe had been wonderful for all of them, but the last of the summer had flown past.

The twins' final days in New York were frantic before leaving for college—packing, organizing everything from computers to bicycles, and seeing all their friends. Ginny was excited to discover that several of her friends had accepted The Arches' invitation and were coming out with her. Veronica continued to pooh-pooh it, and then happened to see the photographs of Ginny in both dresses the day before they left for Brown, when she was looking for stamps in her mother's desk. She stood staring at the photographs for a long moment in outrage, with a look of astonished disbelief.

"How could you do that?" she railed at her mother, and accused her sister of lying to her, and finally Ginny broke down.

"Why should Mom pay both our tuitions because you want to make a statement and are willing to make Dad mad? It's just not fair to her." Veronica had refused to visit Chauncey in Newport that summer, in protest of the position he'd taken. Ginny had dutifully gone there alone the weekend after they got home from Europe. "It's just not right. Why should Mom be punished because you won't do it?" Ginny had finally gotten under her skin, as had Harry's mother, who quietly took Veronica to lunch before they left, and asked her to be a good sport about it. And on her last night in New York, she agreed. Veronica swore she would hate doing it, and still disapproved of it violently, but her father's unreasonable position finally did it for her. She didn't want him to penalize their mother, so she grudgingly agreed. Olympia thanked her profusely, and promised to try and make it as painless as possible for her. Veronica tried on the dress and said she hated it, but it looked spectacular on her. She didn't have an escort yet, but promised to think about it. She had to give the committee his name by Thanksgiving.

"What about one of Charlie's friends?" Olympia suggested, and Veronica said she'd come up with someone herself. It was enough for now that she had agreed to do it, she didn't want to be bugged about her escort, so Olympia backed off. The only remaining protester was Harry, who refused to even discuss the matter with her. He was disappointed that Veronica had conceded, but given her father's manipulative and punitive position, he agreed that it had been the decent thing for her to do, for her mother's sake. But there was no penalty for his not attending. He refused to reconsider, and said nothing on earth could make him go. He was incredibly stubborn about it, and insisted it was a matter of principle. Charlie attempted to broach the subject with him before he left for his senior year at Dartmouth, and Harry changed the subject whenever Charlie mentioned it. It was clear to everyone, including Max, that Harry wouldn't go. Despite the wonderful time they had shared in Europe, Harry hadn't mellowed a bit about the ball.

Olympia and Charlie had lunch together on his last weekend at home, and he seemed relaxed and happy after the summer. He seemed more at ease in his own skin than he had in June, and she was no longer worried about him. He was busy with his friends in the city, said he was looking forward to the school year, and planning to apply to divinity school that fall. He was also talking about doing graduate studies at Oxford, or taking a year off and traveling, or maybe taking a job he'd been offered in San Francisco, working for his roommate's father. He hadn't made his mind up yet about his many options, all of which sounded reasonable to his mother and Harry. She felt sorry for him at times, he seemed so young. It was so hard to make definitive life choices and the right decisions. He was a responsible boy, and a good student, everyone he met liked him. He was thinking about a teaching job, too. He was all over the map.

"Poor kid, I'd hate to be young again," Olympia commented to Harry the day she'd had lunch with Charlie. "He's feeling pulled in about four hundred directions. His father wants him to come to Newport and train polo ponies with him. Thank God that's not one of the options he's considering." Nor was working in Chauncey's family's bank in New York. He had decided against it. Charlie wanted to do something different, he just hadn't figured out what yet. Harry thought he should go to Oxford. Olympia liked the sound of the job in San Francisco. And Charlie himself wasn't sure. Harry had also suggested law school, which Charlie had resisted. He still liked the idea of divinity school best of all. "I can't see him as a minister," Olympia said honestly, although he was religious, more so than the rest of the family.

"Maybe it would suit him," Harry said, looking pensive. "He won't make money at it. It would be nice if he had another option, something a little more profit-oriented." The job in San Francisco was actually in Palo Alto, with a computer company, which Olympia had encouraged him to seriously consider. He was planning to go out and visit his friend and his father after Christmas, after he escorted his sister to the deb ball. The whole family was planning to go to Aspen for Christmas, which sounded like a great idea to all. Before the ball, they would celebrate Chanukah in New York.

The day after Charlie left, Frieda and Olympia went shopping for dresses for the ball. They went to Saks and Bergdorf, and finally found dresses at Barney's that were exactly what they both wanted. A narrow navy satin dress for Olympia with a matching stole, and a black velvet long-sleeved high-necked gown for Frieda, which was flattering, age appropriate, and demure. They returned victorious from their shopping venture. They had tea at Frieda's apartment afterward and chatted like two girls, as they both kicked their shoes off. It seemed as if Frieda was getting more excited hourly about the ball. Now that she had a dress, she could really look forward to it. She said she was going to wear it with the small diamond earrings Harry and Olympia had given her for her seventy-fifth birthday, and a string of pearls from Harry's father.

"I'm worried about Charlie," Olympia admitted, as they sat in Frieda's cozy kitchen. Her house was immaculate, and she was proud of the fact that she still cleaned it herself. She was lively and independent, and proudly refused all of Harry's offers to get help for her. "The poor kid has so many choices about what to do after college. He seems so confused."

"He's still young. He'll find his way. How is his relationship with his father these days?" She knew it had been strained off and on over the past fifteen years. Chauncey was always disappointing. He seemed to be far more interested in the three daughters he had with Felicia than the three children from his previous marriage. The twins didn't seem bothered by it, but Charlie always felt let down by him. Harry did his best to be supportive of him, but Charlie's own father's seeming indifference to him weighed heavily on him. It was just the way Chauncey was. Superficial, with a short attention span, and a strong dislike for responsibility. If it wasn't fun, and couldn't be done on horseback, he didn't do it. He had always wanted Charlie to play polo, and was annoyed he hadn't. Charlie had told Frieda on several occasions that he thought it was a stupid game.

"His relationship with Chauncey is nonexistent," Olympia said, looking troubled. "And Harry is so busy, he doesn't have a lot of time to spend with him. Charlie doesn't open up a lot with anyone these days." She told her then of his friend's suicide the previous spring. "He didn't say much about it, but I got a bill for counseling from Dartmouth, and he said that's why he went. He was still upset when he came home in June. But he was his old self in August when he came back from Colorado."

"Do you think he's okay?" Frieda looked concerned. She had the broad interests and perceptions of a much younger woman, rather than the indifference and fatigue more typical of her age.

"I do," Olympia said cautiously. "I think he's a deep thinker, and keeps a lot to himself. He doesn't confide in me as much as he used to. I guess that's normal, but I worry anyway."

"Does he have a girlfriend?" Frieda had lost track of his pursuits over the summer. He hadn't spent much time in the city after his job in Colorado, before he left to go back to Dartmouth again. Time always moved too quickly, and he'd been busy with friends.

"No one in particular. He went out with a few of Veronica and Ginny's friends this summer. He had a girlfriend sophomore year, but they broke up over Christmas that year. I don't think there's been anyone important since then, and maybe he was too depressed about his friend this spring. He didn't mention meeting anyone important in Colorado this summer. He's pretty picky for a kid his age." Frieda nodded. He was a decent, sensitive, considerate boy, who spent a lot of time with his sisters and brother, had a strong bond to his mother, and a deep affection for Harry. She had a feeling that the ministry really might be the right choice for him. And then she smiled at her daughter-in-law, as she poured them both another cup of tea. They had had a lovely afternoon together, as they always did.

"Maybe he should be a rabbi, instead of a minister. My father was a wonderful rabbi, he was so kind with people, and such a wise, learned man." It was rare that she spoke of her parents, and it always touched Olympia when she did.

"Chauncey would be thrilled." They both laughed at the thought of her snobbish ex-husband's reaction to Charlie converting and becoming a rabbi. "I love the idea. It would drive him insane."

Frieda had only met Chauncey and Felicia once, and he had been barely civil to her. She wasn't even a blip on his radar screen. He had instantly dismissed her, as he did anyone who was not part of his familiar social world. Olympia knew he would be annoyed that she had invited Frieda to The Arches. More than likely, he would ignore her, and he would be even more upset that she had invited Margaret Washington to join them as well. Elderly Jewish women and African Americans were not Chauncey's idea of appropriate guests for a debutante cotillion. It was easy for Olympia to imagine the kind of guests they would bring, if they did. All very Social Register, snobbishly aristocratic, and boring as dirt. At least Frieda was fun and interesting to talk to, she had traveled widely, read constantly, loved to talk politics, and had a warm way with people. And Margaret was one of the smartest people Olympia knew. She was still upset that Harry said he wouldn't be there. He had dug his heels in and refused to discuss it with her. She had given up by then, and Frieda nearly had, too. The ball was still three months away. At least now they both had dresses, as did the girls. The conversation moved on to some of Olympia's cases, and a scandal in the Senate that had recently been in the news.

Olympia didn't leave till nearly dinnertime. When she got home, Harry was cooking dinner, Max was helping him. They had made a huge mess in the kitchen, but they seemed to be having fun. Harry had lit the barbecue in the garden, and they were having steak. Max had just started first grade.

"Where have you been?" Harry inquired as she kissed him and then bent to give her son a hug.

"Shopping with your mother," she said, looking happy to be with them. It was the kind of cozy, domestic scene she loved.

"Was she okay?" he asked, as he put the steaks on a tray. It was still warm outside.

"Fine. We found her a really pretty dress for the ball."

"Oh that," he said, frowning, and then walked outside to put the steaks on the barbecue, as Max turned to his mother.

"He's still not going," Max said with a serious expression.

"I know." Olympia smiled at her youngest son.

"You're not mad at him anymore?" Max was concerned.

"No. He has a right to his opinions." As she said it, Harry walked back in, and she spoke directly to him. "Although your position about not going to the ball is actually discriminatory. You're discriminating against WASPs."

"They're discriminating against blacks and Jews."

"I guess you're even then," she said calmly. "I'm not sure one discrimination is better than the other. It seems about the same to me."

"You've been talking to my mother," he said, tossing the salad. "She just wants an excuse to get dressed up. You all do. You're losing sight of what this kind of thing means."

"It's just a rite of passage, Harry. There's no malice behind it, and the girls will be disappointed if you don't go. That seems worse to me, hurting people you love and who love you, in order to make a statement to people you don't know, and who won't care that you're not there. We will."

"You'll be fine without me. Max and I will stay here."

"What are they going to come out of?" Max asked, still confused about what the girls would be doing, and how Charlie would help them, while his mother and grandmother watched. Although he knew his father disapproved.

"The girls are going to walk out on a big stage, under an archway of flowers, and they will make a curtsy, like this." She demonstrated it for him, sinking gracefully with her head up and back straight, and then coming back up again with her arms extended like a ballerina.

"That's it?" Max looked intrigued, as Harry went to turn the steaks on the barbecue. He had seen her curtsy and pretended he didn't. He didn't want to know.

"That's it. It looks better in a long dress."

"That looked pretty good." Max looked impressed. His mother was pretty, and so were his sisters. He was proud of all of them, and Charlie and his dad, too. "Do the girls know how to do that?" He hadn't seen them practice and it looked hard to him. He suspected correctly that it was harder than it looked.

"Not yet, but they will. They'll have a rehearsal that afternoon before the ball."

"I bet they do it better than everyone else," Max said with certainty. "What will Charlie do?"

"He'll stand next to Ginny while she does it, and then give her his arm, and they'll walk down the stairs. And afterward, the girls will dance with their dad."

"Both of them at the same time?" It sounded complicated to Max.

"No, one at a time." The other twin could have danced with Harry, if he'd been there, and then switched. This way, without him, they would have to take turns.

"Who's going to walk Veronica down the stairs?"

"We don't know yet. Veronica has to figure it out by Thanksgiving."

"He better be good, so he can catch her if she falls over while she does that thing you just did, or if she falls down the stairs." Harry and Olympia both laughed and their eyes met, as he put their steaks on plates. And then suddenly Olympia laughed at the memory of her own escort. She hadn't thought of it in years.

"My date got drunk before we got out onstage. He passed out, and they had to find another boy to go onstage with me. I'd never met him before, but he was very nice."

"I bet they got really mad at the one who got drunk."

"Yes, they did." She remembered, too, and didn't mention, that it had been the last time she danced with her father. He had died the following year, and later she had cherished the bittersweet memory of her last dance with him. It had been an important night for her, just as she hoped it would be for the girls. Not a life-changing moment, but one that, in retrospect, had always meant a lot to her. She had never given it any particular social importance or significance. It had just been a night when she felt special and important, and everyone had made a fuss over her. She had never felt that beautiful again until her wedding day. Other events in her life had had deeper meaning, her marriages to Chauncey and later Harry, the births of her children, her graduation from Vassar and later Columbia Law School, the day she learned she had passed the bar. But that one night at The Arches had meant a lot to her, too. Particularly the last dance with her dad.

"It sounds like a bat mitzvah," Harry said quietly, as he listened to her.

"You're right," she said gently. "It's all about how important a young girl is on that special day." She had been to one or two with him over the years, and had been impressed by how special the girl being celebrated felt, as they made speeches about her, showed films of her childhood, and carried her mother around the room in a chair. Bar mitzvahs, for boys, were even more impressive, and also a rite of passage. They were all-important landmarks between adulthood and youth—officially, the end of your childhood, and your entry into an adult world. Watching Veronica and Virginia go through it was something she would have liked to share with him.

Harry still didn't see it that way. He thought it was more important to make a statement about the political incorrectness of the event. Max asked a number of questions about bar mitzvahs then, and Harry talked about his. It was a time he would always remember with tenderness and joy. Max was already excited thinking about his, and it was seven years away.

The girls called as Olympia and Harry

were cleaning up after dinner. They liked their classes, and said everything was fine at school. They were sharing a suite with each other and two other girls. Charlie had a single room that year, as a lofty senior at Dartmouth. He had opted to live on campus, in the dorms. He had talked about getting a house with a bunch of roommates, and decided against it in the end. He said he didn't mind living in the dorms again. They hadn't heard from him since the day he left. They knew he was busy, and had a lot to do as he started his senior year. None of the older children was coming home before Thanksgiving. It felt like too long to Olympia before she saw them again. It made her more grateful than ever that they had Max, and another twelve years to look forward to with him.

Harry and Olympia put Max to bed together that night. Harry read him a story, while Olympia kissed him and tucked him in. After they did, they went to their own room, and talked for a long time. They both had heavy workloads and important cases to deal with. They liked talking about their work and the things they did all day. She loved sharing all aspects of her life with him, and hearing what he thought. She valued his opinions and judgment, about all matters, except the deb ball. She thought he was being utterly absurd about that.

When she snuggled up next to him in bed that night, she was grateful for him. She loved the life and children they shared. It was a good life, filled with loving people, work they enjoyed, and children who were a perpetual blessing to them. She fell asleep in his arms as they whispered, and for the first time in months, the ball no longer seemed important, whether or not he attended. If not, it no longer mattered. She loved him anyway.

Chapter 4

All of the children came home for Thanksgiving. Charlie came home on Tuesday, the girls on Wednesday. They had just gone through the agony of midterms, and all three of the older children felt liberated and free. Max was thrilled to have them too, and loved playing with them. Charlie picked him up at school the day he got home, and took him to Central Park, to the zoo. He bought him hot chestnuts and a balloon. And the following afternoon, he took him skating. They returned with pink cheeks, bright eyes, and in great spirits. By the time they got home, the girls had arrived, and they shared a lively dinner before Charlie and the twins went out afterward to meet their friends. Their noisy presence in the house reminded

Olympia of how much she loved having all of her children at home.

On Thanksgiving morning Frieda arrived in time to help Olympia with dinner. Harry had made the stuffing, Olympia cooked the turkey, Frieda did the vegetables, Charlie made the corn muffins, the girls made sweet potatoes with marshmallows, and Olympia helped Max make whipped cream, to serve on the apple and pumpkin pies at the end of the meal. It was the one meal of the year when everyone contributed and made an effort, and the end result was stupendous. They sat down to dinner at six, and by eight o'clock, everyone was so stuffed, they couldn't move. And, as she always did, Olympia had provided a kosher meal just for Frieda, prepared by a kosher caterer the day before, which she said had been delicious too.

"I'm going to have to starve for the next three weeks, so I can get into my dress," Frieda commented, after eating the pumpkin pie with the whipped cream on it that had been Max's contribution to the meal.

"Me too," Ginny said, looking worried. Veronica had announced earlier that she had invited a boy called Jeff Adams to be her escort. She said she had met him at school. He was coming down for the weekend of the ball, and he had promised to rent a tux in Providence and bring it with him, so he didn't need to rent one in New York.

"I hope he's reliable," Olympia said, looking slightly worried. "How well do you know him?"

"Well enough," Veronica said casually. "I've been going out with him for about three weeks."

"What happens if you stop dating him before the cotillion? That could be awkward." Everyone always agreed that boyfriends made bad escorts, because if you stopped seeing them just before the ball, you could wind up without a date.

"He's just a friend," Veronica said, looking unconcerned. She had agreed to make her debut, but without any enthusiasm. She was only doing it so her father wouldn't withdraw his share of the tuition for school. But she was still angry about his blackmail and manipulation. She had told everyone repeatedly that she fully anticipated having a rotten time at the ball. She was the original reluctant debutante, but Ginny more than made up for what her twin sister lacked in excitement about the event. She couldn't wait, and had tried on her dress four times in the last two days. It was the ballgown of her dreams. Charlie had checked the night he got back, and said his tuxedo still fit, although he said it was a little tight in the waist, but nothing he couldn't live with for one night.

Veronica had said that her escort wanted to meet Charlie and Ginny, but he had gone skiing in Vermont over the Thanksgiving weekend.

"What's he like?" Charlie asked with interest. It would be more fun for all of them if the two escorts got along and had something in common to chat about at the rehearsal and ball. It was going to be a long evening for them.

"He's on the football team, and he plays ice hockey, too," Veronica told her brother.

"Maybe we can all go skating the next day," Charlie said hopefully, "or to dinner or something. Is he excited to do it?"

"I don't know. I asked. He said he would. He doesn't have to love it. All he has to do is be there." Veronica dismissed the possibility of his enjoying it, since she knew she wouldn't. In her opinion, neither would he.

"Has he ever been an escort at a deb ball before?" their mother inquired, as Veronica looked at her belligerently.

"I don't know. Why would he? Once would be enough for me."

"Some guys actually enjoy it," Olympia informed her, "hard as you may find that to believe." She smiled at her, glad that she had finally agreed.

"I do find it hard to believe. It sounds like a major drag to me."

"You may be pleasantly surprised by how much fun it is," her mother said encouragingly, as Ginny smiled from ear to ear. She had been able to think of nothing else for the past many weeks.

Harry's mother stayed until nearly midnight. He put her in a cab and sent her home, and as he went out to help her, he saw that it was snowing.

By morning, the city was blanketed by snow. After lunch they all agreed to go to Central Park, and when they did, they wrapped garbage bags around their bottoms, and slid down the hills. Max rapidly became an expert at it, and Harry wasn't bad at it, either. It was a lot of fun, and Olympia laughed with pleasure as she slid down the hills. The girls lay in the snow, and made angels by waving their arms as far up and down as they could, making impressions that looked like wings in the fresh snow. They had been doing that since they were little children, and loved it more than ever. Afterward, they all went to Rockefeller Center, skated, and had dinner. After they got back to the house, they called their friends, figured out plans, and the three oldest ones went out shortly after to meet up with people, or hang out in their homes. Max was sound asleep by the time they left, exhausted after a long, busy day. He had worn himself out making a snowman with his older brother.

"It's been a wonderful Thanksgiving," Olympia said to Harry as they got into bed and slid under the sheets. "It's so nice to have the kids home. I miss them so much when they're gone." He knew she did. "I can't wait till they come home for winter break." They were scheduled to come home the week before the ball. The ball he still refused to go to, and that Margaret Washington and Frieda were attending with her. Much as she loved them both, she would have preferred to have Harry at her side than them. But it was still not an option, as far as he was concerned. He was absolutely immovable about not going. He was making a statement about an event he profoundly disapproved of, and what he perceived as their discriminatory practices, by not attending, no matter how much it upset his wife. This was one time he was willing to upset her, and felt he had to, in order to be true to what he believed. In fact, no one cared if he went or not, except Olympia and his family.

The big announcement of the weekend was made by Virginia on Saturday morning. She had debated about telling them and, after a long cozy heart-to-heart with her mother after breakfast, decided she should. She never kept secrets from her, and loved sharing all the details of her life. Olympia had suspected something was going on with her, but as she no longer saw her every day, it was hard to find the right opportunity for Ginny to confide in her. Their after-breakfast chat gave Ginny the chance she needed to spill the beans. She was madly in love with a junior at Brown she said. He was the coolest boy she'd ever met. Like the boy Veronica was dating and bringing to the ball, he was on the football team. His name was Steve, and Ginny was head over heels in love with him, unlike Veronica, who liked her date, but for the moment was nothing more than friends with him. Ginny told her mother she had been seeing him three or four times a week for three months. And she asked if he could come to the ball, too. Olympia had reserved a table, and said she would save a seat for him. Ginny was thrilled. Since her brother was her official escort, there was no conflict in having Steve there, too. She said he was from Boston, from a very respectable family. He was a twin, too, and his brother was at Duke. From everything she said to Olympia, he sounded like a nice kid.

Olympia told Harry about it that afternoon, and said she was pleased for her, although she hoped Ginny's studies wouldn't suffer from the amount of time she was spending with him. Ginny had said they studied together, and spent a lot of time in the library when he wasn't at practice with the team. "She's so crazy about him, it's really cute."

Olympia looked delighted. Ginny had had a number of crushes in high school, and several boyfriends. Her romances usually lasted a few months. Veronica was much slower about getting involved, and had a much longer list of requirements. Most of the time, she went out with friends, and had been in love only once. She was more cautious by nature, and more intellectual. The girls looked totally identical, but were completely different in disposition. Olympia asked Veronica about Steve later that afternoon, and she said he was okay, but didn't seem enthused.

"You don't sound too thrilled," Olympia commented with concern. Veronica wasn't jealous by nature, and she wondered if something was wrong, or if he was less of a catch than Ginny said.

"Steve's okay, he's kind of the hot guy on campus, or thinks he is. A lot of girls are always chasing after him. He's pretty full of himself." That kind of narcissistic personality never appealed much to her.

"Is he as nuts about Ginny as she is about him?" Olympia was worried by what Veronica had said.

"He says he is," Veronica said coolly. She had a much more wait-and-see attitude about life, and was far more cynical and cautious than her more exuberant sister. "I don't like guys who are that handsome. Sometimes they're weird." She liked the interesting, more unusual ones, who were better to talk to than to look at. The boys Ginny went out with were always strikingly good-looking. In some ways, they always reminded Olympia a little of Chauncey, as though Ginny were looking for a younger version of her elusive, inattentive father. And it sounded as though she was head over heels in love with Steve.

Virginia had admitted to her mother that they were sleeping together, but had promised her that they always used protection. But the degree of her infatuation with him worried her mother anyway, particularly after what Veronica said.

"I get the feeling you don't like him," Olympia said honestly, fishing for more reasons why, if not.

"He's okay. I'm not crazy about him. Someone told me he jerks girls around a lot. I don't want her to get hurt," Veronica said honestly, with worried eyes. But once Ginny got an idea in her head, she was hard to stop. About anything. Veronica was stubborn, too, though usually about ideas, not people.

"I don't want her to get hurt either," Olympia said. Ginny was obviously moving full steam ahead. "Keep an eye on her, please. Talk sense to her, if you need to," Olympia said conspiratorially, as Veronica laughed and rolled her eyes.

"Yeah. Sure. A lot of good that would do me with Ginny. You know how she is." Mostly, with Ginny, all you could do was help her pick up the pieces later. When she fell, she fell hard. And when it was over, her whole world came crashing down around her. In some ways, Veronica was tougher and more solid. Olympia knew her children well.

"What about you? Anything serious going on with this Jeff you invited to be your escort?"

"Nope," Veronica said noncommittally. She was always very closed about her love life, even with her mother, and sometimes even with Ginny. She kept her own counsel, as did Charlie. They were both much more like their father than their mother on that issue. Ginny and Olympia were far more open, and willing to tell all. Olympia kept no secrets, nor did Ginny. They wore their hearts on their sleeves at all times. Harry loved that about her. It was one of the many reasons why he had fallen in love with her in the first place. "He's just a guy, we're friends," Veronica said about Jeff.

"What made you invite him to the ball?" Olympia asked, curious about him, and somewhat nervous. There was no telling if Veronica would do something to sabotage her attendance at the event. It wouldn't be unlike her. Olympia was afraid to press her about it, and make her balk again.

"I had to invite someone. Everyone else I know would laugh me out of the room if I asked them. His sister came out last year, he thought it was stupid, too. So I figured he wouldn't laugh at me if I asked him. We agree, it's a dumb thing to do. But he said he'd do it." He had also said they could get stoned before they went on stage for her to make her bow. But she didn't share that piece of information with her mother. She thought it was funny, whether they did it or not.

"Does he look normal?" Olympia asked with some trepidation, as Veronica gave her a dark look, with obvious irritation.

"No, Mom, he has three heads, and a bone through his nose. Yeah, he looks normal, most of the time. He knows the drill. He'll look fine that night."

"What does he look like the rest of the time?" Olympia asked gingerly.

"Sort of punk, but nothing too outrageous. He spikes his hair, but he said he didn't for his sister's debut. He'll be fine, Mom. Don't worry."

"I hope so," Olympia said with a sigh. She was beginning to feel stressed about the event, and she wouldn't have Harry to lean on. She, Frieda, Margaret Washington and her husband, another couple, Ginny's new boyfriend Steve, and Chauncey and Felicia would be sharing a table. A motley crew at best. The debutantes and their escorts would be seated elsewhere.

Olympia mentioned her concerns to Charlie before he went back to school, and he assured his mother everything would be all right. It was only one evening. Nothing much was going to happen. The girls would make their bow. They would parade around the room. Their father would dance with them, and the rest of the evening would be spent eating, drinking, and dancing. What could go wrong?

"You make it sound so simple." She

smiled at her firstborn. He had that way about him. Charlie always put oil on troubled waters, and calmed her down. He had always been a great comfort to her. He never made waves himself, instead he smoothed things over when others did, as occasionally happened in any family. He was the peacemaker in their midst, the ever-responsible oldest child, trying to be all that his father was not.

"It is simple," he said with a warm smile, but behind the smile, once again she saw sadness, as she had since the previous spring, when his friend died.

"Are you okay?" She looked deep into his eyes and could not decipher what she saw there. She sensed more than saw that something was hidden. She hoped nothing was wrong in his life. He was a deep thinker, and had been even as a young child.

"I'm fine, Mom."

"Sure? Are you happy at school?"

"Happy enough, and I'm almost finished." She knew he was worrying a lot about what to do when he graduated in June. He was still planning to go to California, to interview with his friend's father. He had decided not to go after Christmas, and to go over spring break instead. He had also applied to Oxford for a year of graduate studies, before applying to divinity school at Harvard. He had options and choices, and decisions to make, which was stressful for him. He had his whole life ahead of him to work out. It was always important to Charlie to feel he was doing the right thing.

"Don't worry too much about what you're going to do. You'll figure it out. The right thing will just happen. Give it time."

"I know it will be okay, Mom." He leaned over and kissed her. "Don't you worry, either. Have you talked to Dad lately?"

She shook her head. "Not since last summer, when he was so mad at Veronica saying she wouldn't come out."

"Maybe you should just call him to say hi, so it's not too awkward that night." He knew how much his mother disliked Felicia, and how strained her relationship had become with Chauncey. They had absolutely nothing in common.

It was a mystery to all the children how their parents had ever gotten married. Seven years together was remarkable between people who were that mismatched, although at twenty-two Olympia had been a different person. She had been a product of her own very conservative Episcopalian upbringing, and Chauncey's Social Register world had been familiar to her. Charlie had always suspected that she had married him because her parents died when she was in college, and she was looking for stability and a family, so she had gotten married. But as she evolved over the years, and developed her own ideas and way of thinking, they had grown apart. Now they lived on separate planets. Charlie thought his mother's world more interesting. He liked Harry a lot, he had always been wonderful to him. But he also had deep affection and loyalty to his father, whatever his quirks, prejudices, failures, and limitations. And Felicia was just silly. Charlie thought she was harmless. His mother had never agreed with him. She thought that Chauncey's wife was a living monument to stupidity and malice. Mostly because Felicia was wildly jealous of her, and never failed to make some incredibly dumb comment when they saw each other, which was rare enough. He knew that it was going to be hard for his mom not to have Harry with her, and was sorry that Harry couldn't get over his own principles to be there for her. But apparently, that wasn't going to happen. Charlie had promised himself, as always, that he would do everything he could to help her, in Harry's absence. And his suggestion to call Chauncey, to pave the way for a peaceful evening, was a good one. He knew his father would be flattered by the call. Chauncey liked homage and attention.

"Maybe I will call him," Olympia said cautiously. She wasn't enthused about it, but recognized it as a diplomatic suggestion. "Are you going up to see him over Christmas break?"

"I thought I'd go up for a couple of days, before we go to Aspen." Harry, Olympia, and all the children were going to Colorado over Christmas for a week of skiing, as they did every year. They all looked forward to it. Charlie never admitted it to anyone, but it was more fun being with them than with his father. But he went to see him out of loyalty and affection, and always the hope that they would be able to connect somehow, at a deeper level. So far that had never happened. Chauncey wasn't a deep person. "He has some new polo ponies he wants to show me." Charlie looked sad as he said it. He knew what a disappointment it was to his father that he didn't want to play polo. He liked riding with him, and had ridden to hounds with him in Europe, just to see what it was like, but polo bored him. It was his father's passion.

"Do you want to bring any friends with you to Aspen?" They rented a house there, and Olympia was always open to the kids bringing friends with them. It was more fun for them if they did, but Charlie shook his head, after a flicker of hesitation.

"No, I'll ski with the girls, or Harry." Olympia stayed on the bunny slopes with Max. The others were much wilder skiers than she was, particularly Charlie.

"If you change your mind, that's fine. There's plenty of room if you want to bring a couple of buddies from Dartmouth. A girl would be okay, too." She smiled at him. If he brought a girl, she would room with Veronica and Ginny. They had big, wholesome, friendly family vacations, and all were welcome.

"If I find a girl to bring, I'll tell you." He had no big romance at the moment. Not since the one sophomore year, and several in high school. But for the past two years, there had been no one special, and still wasn't. He was cautious and discerning. Olympia always said that it was going to take a special girl, with many qualities and considerable depth, to win Charlie. He was the most serious of all her children. It was hard to believe at times that he was related to Chauncey, who was the king of all things superficial.

He flew back to Dartmouth that night, and the girls went back to Brown in the morning. They didn't start school till Tuesday. Ginny tried her dress on one last time before she left, and stood beaming at herself in the mirror. She loved it. Olympia had to threaten Veronica's life to try hers on, but she wanted to be sure it fit, and needed no alterations before the big night. When they came home in December, there wouldn't be time to alter it before the rehearsal and ball.

"You both have shoes, right?" Ginny had bought hers in July, perfectly plain white satin pumps, with little pearls on them, just like her dress. They had been lucky to find them. Veronica insisted she had a pair of white satin evening sandals in her closet.

"You're sure?" Olympia asked again. They both had evening bags, long white kid gloves, and the string of pearls with matching earrings she had bought each of them for their eighteenth birthdays. That was all they needed.

"I'm sure," Veronica said, rolling her eyes. "Do you realize how much more worthwhile it would be if we spent the money on people who are starving in Appalachia?"

"The two are not mutually exclusive. Harry and I give plenty of money to charity, Veronica. He does more pro bono work than anyone I know, and I do my share. You don't need to feel guilty over one dress and a pair of sandals."

"I'd rather spend the night working in a homeless shelter."

"That's noble of you. You can atone for your sins when we get back from Aspen." They had a month's vacation, and she was sure that Veronica would be doing just that for most of her vacation. She had volunteered many times in homeless shelters, with literacy projects, and with abused kids at a center she loved in Harlem. No one had ever accused Veronica of lacking social conscience. Ginny was another story. She would spend her month's vacation seeing friends, going to parties, and shopping.

All Olympia wanted was for her children to love and respect each other, however different they were. And so far her encouragement in that direction had been successful. In spite of their disagreement about the debut ball, the girls were as devoted to each other and to Charlie and Max as the boys were to them.

Olympia went back to her office the next morning when the girls left. Harry had gone to work early. The school bus had picked Max up, and she had a thousand messages on her desk when she got there. She waded through them and returned all her calls, before a court appearance that afternoon. During her lunch break, she called Chauncey. She had thought Charlie's suggestion was a good one, just to break the ice, and try and get things on an easy footing, which was never simple for her with Chauncey. He had an unfailing ability to irritate her.

Felicia answered the phone in Newport, and she and Olympia chatted for a few minutes, about nothing in particular, mostly Felicia and Chauncey's children. She was complaining about their school in Newport, and how stupid it was that they had to wear uniforms, instead of the cute little outfits she bought them in Boston and New York. She was nice enough to say though that she was looking forward to the girls' debut at The Arches, and Olympia thanked her and asked for Chauncey. Felicia said he had just come in for lunch, from the stables. It still amazed Olympia that her ex-husband had been content not to work for the past fifteen years, and live off his family fortune. She couldn't imagine a life like that, even if she could afford it. She loved her law practice, and respected Harry for all he had accomplished. In his entire lifetime, Chauncey had achieved nothing. All he did was play polo, and buy horses. In their early days together, he had worked in his family's bank, but he had given that up quickly. It took too much effort, and was too much trouble. Now he made no pretense about the indolent life he led, and always jokingly said that work was for the masses. He was a snob to his core.

He sounded out of breath when he came on the line. He had run up from the stables, and was surprised when Felicia told him Olympia was calling. Unless something dire was happening, she never called him.

Whatever plans or information she needed to share, she sent by e-mail.

"Something wrong?" he asked, sounding worried. She would have had the same reaction if he called. Chatty calls were unheard of between them. Neither of them was interested in social contact with each other. He couldn't understand the choices she'd made, to go to law school, and marry a Jew. And she had even less respect for how he chose to lead his life, and with whom. She thought Felicia was a moron. But like it or not, she and Chauncey shared three children, which forced them to have some contact with each other, if only on state occasions, like the girls' debut. Later on there would be weddings, shared grandchildren, and christenings. To Olympia, it was not a cheering prospect. Nor to him. He had developed a profound dislike for her over the years, and couldn't imagine why he had married her, either.

"No. Everything's fine. I didn't mean to worry you. I just wanted to touch base before the big night. I can't believe it's almost here. Where will you be staying?"

"At Felicia's brother's apartment. He's in Europe." Olympia had heard years before that it was a palatial penthouse on Fifth Avenue, with a breathtaking view of the park, and a glass dome over a hot tub on the terrace. He was a perennial bachelor and only slightly older than Felicia. He was best known for dating Hollywood starlets, and European princesses. The girls had been impressed by his Ferrari when they last saw him.

"That should be nice," Olympia said benignly. "Will you be here for long?" She wondered if she should invite them to the house for drinks, but cringed at the prospect, and she knew Harry would, too. The two men grudgingly acknowledged each other. Harry was polite to him, but Chauncey was barely civil. He ignored him.

"Just the weekend. Is Veronica behaving?" Chauncey asked with interest.

"Seems like it. She finally lined up an escort. Some boy called Jeff Adams. She swears he's respectable. I hope she's right."

"If he's not, or looks like hell, the committee will kick him out at the rehearsal. Any idea who his parents are?" He didn't ask if Jeff's parents were in the Social Register, but Olympia knew he'd like to.

"None. All she said is that his sister came

out last year," which meant that he would pass muster for Chauncey. That was all it took. The criteria were simple for him.

"Ask her what his father's name is. I can look them up in the Social Register, maybe I know them." For once, it might be reassuring. The Social Register ran Chauncey's life, the way some people's were ruled by the Bible. It was his Bible. Olympia didn't even own one, although years before her family had been in it. They had dropped her when she married Harry and disappeared off the fancy social scene forever. She had pretty much done that when she left Chauncey. They had kept her name in for a couple of years after that, as a courtesy, and then her name was withdrawn when she remarried. Chauncey had considered that a major tragedy. Olympia thought it was funny.

"I don't think I want to ruffle Veronica's feathers any more than they already are. I'm just grateful she's agreed to do it."

"I should hope so," he said, sounding as though they had averted a major tragedy, or a near drowning. He couldn't even imagine having a daughter who didn't make her debut. It would have been a disaster in his life. "They have dresses, I assume," he said, trying to maintain the banter she was keeping up. He was stunned that she had called him, for apparently no important reason, and he thought it suspicious, but if truly benign, then it was very nice of her. Usually, when they had contact, it was over some dispute, and she was feisty with him.

"They'll both look beautiful," Olympia assured him. "The dresses are lovely."

"I'm not surprised," he said charitably. "You have a good eye." Better than Felicia, he knew. Olympia had impeccable taste. Felicia's was a little fluffy, though he would never have said that to either wife. "Is your husband coming?" He had no idea why he had asked her that, it seemed obvious that he would, and Chauncey was surprised when she hesitated.

"No, actually. He isn't. He has some family event he has to go to," and then she remembered that Frieda would be there, and decided to be honest with him. "Actually, that's not true. He thinks the whole idea is politically incorrect, and excludes people of other races and colors, so he's not coming."

"That's too bad for you," he said, sounding sympathetic for once. "Felicia and I will look out for you." It was the nicest he had been in years, and Olympia was glad that she had followed Charlie's suggestion. It warmed things up a bit and broke the ice before the inevitable stresses and tensions of the big night. The girls would be nervous wrecks, and she suspected she would be, too, getting them ready, getting them there, and making sure that all was right. Not to mention an escort for Veronica whom she'd never met, and her attitude about the event. Olympia realized it was still possible, right up to the last second, for Veronica to back out. She just hoped she wouldn't, and had already told Harry several times not to stir her up, or encourage her to do anything foolish. He had promised he wouldn't.

"Anything I can do for you before you come?" Olympia asked generously. "I have a good hairdresser, if Felicia needs one. If she'd like, I can make an appointment for her."

"I think she has one, but thanks. Take care of yourself, Olympia, don't let the girls drive you nuts. We'll see you there."

A moment later they hung up and she sat staring at the phone. She was so distracted she didn't see Margaret walk in with a stack of briefs in her arms.

"You look like you've just seen a boa constrictor sitting on your desk. Everything all right?"

"I think so. More like a boa constrictor in sheep's clothing. Charlie suggested I call his father before the ball. I just did. I can't believe how nice he was." Olympia looked genuinely startled. He was being much nicer about the ball than Harry. But then again, this was Chauncey's kind of event, and surely not Harry's.

"Old boa constrictors die hard," Margaret said with a grin.

"I guess so. He hasn't been that pleasant in fifteen years. I guess he's pleased that the girls are coming out. It's a big deal to him."

"It *is* a big deal. It should be fun for them. Maybe even for you, too. I'm looking forward to it. I've never been to a coming-out ball before. I even bought a new dress."

"Me too." Olympia smiled, grateful for her friend's support. It was more than she could say for Harry. It was a shame he felt he had to make such an issue of it. The only one it hurt was her.

"Has Harry backed down yet?" Margaret asked cautiously, setting the briefs down on

Olympia's desk. She wanted her opinion on them.

"No. I don't think he will. We all worked on him about it. I've finally given up. At least for once Chauncey isn't being a horse's ass. Although God knows how he'll be that night." He tended to drink a lot, although less than when he'd been married to her, according to friends. In his youth, he had been drunk for most of their marriage. In the early days, it made him charming and amorous. Later, he turned surly and nasty. It was impossible to predict how he'd behave with four martinis and a bottle of wine in him on the night of the ball, or worse yet, once he got into the brandy. But for the moment at least, he was being civil, and it was Felicia's problem now to control him once he got drunk. No longer hers, thank God. Felicia drank a lot, too. They had that in common. Olympia had never been much of a drinker, nor was Harry.

"Don't worry, Ollie. I'll be there to hold your hand," Margaret reassured her.

"I'll need it," Olympia said, as she pulled the briefs toward her, across her desk, and Margaret sat down to review them with her. Olympia wasn't sure why, but in spite of her pleasant exchange with Chauncey, she had the feeling that the night of her daughters' debut at The Arches was going to be even more challenging than she feared. Especially without Harry for support.

Chapter 5

The weekend before the coming-out ball, Olympia woke up with a raging fever. She'd been feeling funny for two days. She had a scratchy throat, a stomachache, a stuffy nose, and by Saturday night, she felt like death. Her fever was 102. She was slightly better on Sunday, but the stomachache was worse. She was practically in tears when she came downstairs on Sunday morning. Harry was making breakfast for Max, and she noticed that her son's face was bright red. She took Max's temperature right after breakfast. His was 103, and he said his tummy itched. When she looked, she saw that he had a nasty rash. It was coming up in tiny blisters, and when she took out her trusty copy of Dr. Spock, which she had kept since Charlie was born, what Max had perfectly matched the description of chicken pox, as she suspected.

"Shit!" she said, as she closed the book. This was not the week for either of them to be sick. She had to have all her wits about her, she had a mountain of new cases in the office, and Margaret had taken the week off. And she hated leaving Max with a sitter when he was sick, if she was even going to be well enough to go to work herself. She called the pediatrician, who told her to soak Max in the tub with a powder he recommended, use lots of calamine, and keep him in bed. There was nothing else they could do. Luckily, her own fever abated on Sunday night. She still felt terrible, but at least hers was only the flu, or a bad cold, and hopefully would be gone in a few days. Charlie was due home on Tuesday night, and could help her with Max. The girls were coming home on Wednesday afternoon. Ginny called her late Sunday night. She sounded awful. She said she had bronchitis, she sounded like she was dying of consumption as she coughed into the phone.

"Stay in bed tomorrow," her mother

warned her. For the moment, she sounded too sick to fly home.

"I can't, I have finals," Ginny said, and promptly burst into tears.

"Can you ask them to give you makeup exams?" Olympia suggested. "You sound too sick to go out."

"Makeups are on Friday. If I do that, I won't be home till Friday night." She sobbed miserably. She felt awful, and didn't want to miss the ball that weekend.

"You may not have any other choice than to take makeup exams."

"What if I have a red nose?"

"That's the least of it. Go to the infirmary tomorrow, and see if they'll put you on antibiotics so you don't wind up with an infection and get really sick. That should help." She had gotten them both meningitis shots before they went off to school in September, so at least she knew it wasn't anything worse than a bad cold or at worst bronchitis, and antibiotics would keep it from turning into pneumonia. Ginny sounded just terrible. So far, Veronica hadn't caught it, but sharing a tiny room with her sister, it wasn't going to surprise Olympia if she got sick, too. "Max has chicken pox," her mother said mournfully. "Thank God all of you have had it. That's all we'd need. The poor kid feels awful, too. We're a mess," Olympia said ruefully. It was turning into a hell of a week, with invalids everywhere.

On Monday, she felt better, Max felt worse, and Ginny called to say they had given her antibiotics, so Olympia was hopeful she'd feel better by the end of the week. She'd gone to take her exams and burst into tears when she called her mother, and said she was sure that she had failed. She managed to squeeze in the information that her hot new romance, Steve, was being a jerk, but he said he was still coming to the ball. It sounded like a mixed blessing to her mother, but she didn't have time to ask for the details. The sitter had just come for Max, and sick or not, she had to go to work.

Olympia sat at her desk blowing her nose all day. The stomachache was better, her nose was running, she had a headache, and she had ordered containers of chicken soup from a nearby deli throughout the day. She called the sitter every hour, who told her that Max was all right, but by the end of the day, he was covered with spots. Clearly, it was going to be a challenging week.

It had started to snow that morning, and by afternoon, there were five inches of snow blanketing the city. It said on the radio that the schools would be closed the next day. They were expecting ten more inches during the night, and declared it a blizzard by five o'clock. Olympia thought briefly about calling her mother-in-law to ask her if she needed anything. She didn't want her to go out and fall on the ice as the temperature dropped that night. She dialed her number, there was no answer, and Olympia didn't get out of the office herself till after six that night. She nearly froze to death looking for a cab, and by the time she got home she was soaking wet, and chilled to the bone. Max was propped up in bed, watching videos, and covered in calamine lotion.

"Hi, sweetheart, how's it going?"

"Itchy," he said, looking unhappy. His fever had gone up again, but at least Olympia's hadn't. She had had a miserable, stressful day in the office. And Harry had left a message at the house that he had an emergency at work, and wouldn't be home till at least nine. She couldn't wait for Charlie to come home the next day, and at least give her a hand in cheering up Max, who looked sick, feverish, and bored. Charlie was terrific with him, and Olympia was feeling overwhelmed. It didn't help that Harry was out when she felt sick herself.

She made chicken soup for herself and Max, put a frozen pizza in the microwave for him, and blew her nose about four hundred times. She had just tucked him in for the night, turned off his light, and walked into her bedroom, longing for a hot bath, when the phone rang. It was still snowing heavily outside. It was Frieda, who apologized for calling her. She knew Max had chicken pox, and inquired how he was.

"Poor kid, he looks awful. He's covered with calamine. I didn't think that many spots could fit on one child. He even has them inside his ears, nose, and mouth."

"Poor thing. How's your cold?"

"Miserable," Olympia admitted. "I hope I get rid of it by Saturday night."

"Yes, so do I," Frieda said, sounding vague. And for the first time ever, Olympia had the impression that her mother-in-law was drunk. She hadn't noticed it at first, but she was definitely slurring her words. For an instant, Olympia was afraid she'd had a stroke. She'd had a heart attack five years before, but had been fine ever since.

"Are you all right?" Olympia asked, sounding worried.

"Yes . . . yes . . . I am . . ." She hesitated, and her daughter-in-law could hear a tremor in her voice. "I had a little mishap this afternoon," she said, sounding embarrassed. She loved her independence, managed well on her own, and never liked to be a burden to anyone. She rarely told anyone when she was sick, but only reported on it days or weeks later.

"What kind of mishap?" Olympia asked, blowing her nose.

There was a long pause, and for a moment, Olympia was afraid she'd fallen asleep. She definitely sounded drunk.

"Frieda?" Olympia roused her, and heard her stir at the other end.

"Sorry . . . I'm feeling a little drowsy. I went to get some groceries before the storm got worse. I slipped on the ice. But I'm fine now." She didn't sound it.

"What happened? Did you get hurt?"

"Nothing serious," Frieda reassured her. "I'll be fine in a few days."

"How fine? Did you see a doctor?"

There was another long pause before she answered. "I broke my ankle," she said, sounding chagrined and feeling foolish. "I fell on a patch of ice on the curb. It was such a stupid thing. I should know better."

"Oh my God, how awful. Did you go to the hospital? Why didn't you call me?"

"I know how busy you are at work. I didn't want to bother you. I called Harry, but I couldn't get through. He was in a meeting."

"He still is," Olympia said, obviously distressed over her mother-in-law's accident, and that she hadn't been there to help. "You should have called me, Frieda." She hated the thought of the older woman negotiating the emergency room alone.

"They put me in an ambulance and took me to NYU." It had been quite an adventure, and she had been there all afternoon.

"Are you in a cast?" Olympia was horrified. What had happened to Frieda was far worse than Max's chicken pox, Ginny's cough, or her cold.

"Up to my knee."

"How did you get home?"

"I'm not."

"You're *not*? Where are you?" The story was getting worse by the minute.

"I'm still at the hospital. They didn't want me to go home alone. I'll be on crutches for a few weeks. I'm just lucky I didn't break a hip."

"Oh my God! Frieda! I'm coming to get you. You can stay here with us."

"I don't want to be a burden. I'll be fine tomorrow. And I'm still coming to the ball!"

"Of course you are. We'll get you a wheelchair," Olympia said, suddenly thinking of the logistics of getting her there. Nothing in life was easy, particularly at this time of year.

"I'll walk," Frieda said staunchly, although they had already told her that she wouldn't be able to put weight on her left foot for several weeks. She was going to have to hop around, with the crutches. But she was still determined not to be a problem for anyone. As always, she was sure she could manage on her own.

"You can stay here tonight. You've had chicken pox, right?"

"I think so. I'm not worried about that." Olympia knew that for elderly people, exposure to chicken pox could sometimes result in shingles. But they couldn't leave her alone at home. She might fall and break something else. She had to stay with them.

"I don't want to bother you and the children," Frieda said, and as Olympia listened, she realized they must have given her something for the pain.

"You're not a bother, and there's no reason for you to stay there. Will they let you leave tonight?"

"I think so," Frieda said vaguely.

"I'll call and ask the nurse, and call you back." Olympia took down the details of her room number, the section of the hospital she was in, and the nurses' station that was nearest to her. Although she had obviously been sedated, she was remarkably coherent, and kept apologizing for being a pain in the neck. "You're not," Olympia assured her, and hung up. She tried calling Harry at the office, but his private line was on voicemail, and his secretary had left. It was after eight o'clock.

She called the hospital, and they assured her that Mrs. Rubinstein was doing fine, they had only kept her there for the night so she wouldn't be alone at home. They had given her Vicodin for the considerable pain she was in, but there was no medical reason why she couldn't leave. For a woman her age, she was in remarkably good health, and had been fully coherent when she came in. The nurse on duty said she was a dear. Olympia agreed, and then called the sitter and asked her if she could come back for an hour. Fortunately, she lived nearby, and twenty minutes later she was back. Olympia had told her what had happened, and while she waited for the sitter, she turned the den on the main floor into a bedroom for Frieda. It had a bathroom, TV, and a pull-out bed, as they occasionally used it as a guest room. For as long as was necessary, Frieda could stay with them. She was sure it would be what Harry wanted, too. By eight-thirty, she was out the door, and an hour later they were back. Harry was still out.

She settled Frieda comfortably in the den-turned-guest-room, brought her something to eat, turned on the TV, fluffed up her pillows, took her to the bathroom, supporting most of her weight as she navigated the crutches, and settled her into bed. By ten o'clock, Olympia was upstairs in her own room, when Harry came home. He walked into their bedroom, looking exhausted. He had had an incredibly difficult day, with a case that had attracted national press, a headache he and the other judges involved didn't need.

"Who's in the den?" He assumed it was one of Charlie's friends. They used the room for overflow when all the kids were home. It was the only guest room they had.

"Your mother," Olympia said, blowing her nose for the thousandth time. After negotiating the blizzard again, her cold had gotten markedly worse.

"My mother? What's she doing here?" He looked confused.

"She broke her ankle. They took her to NYU in an ambulance, and she didn't even call me. I just picked her up half an hour ago."

"Are you serious?" He looked stunned.

"I am." She blew her nose yet again. "She can't stay at her place alone. She's in a cast and on crutches. I think she should stay here for a while."

Harry smiled lovingly at his wife. Olympia never let him down. "Is she awake?"

"She was a few minutes ago, but she's pretty looped on the stuff they gave her for the pain. Poor thing, it must have hurt like hell. I told her to call us on the intercom if she needs to, and not to try and go to the bathroom by herself. You know her. She'll be cooking us all breakfast in the morning. We're going to have to tie her to the bed."

"I'll go down and check on her," he said, looking concerned, and then turned to look at Olympia again as he headed out the door. "I love you. Thank you for being so good to her."

Olympia smiled back at him. "She's the only mom we've got."

"You're the best wife in the world."

He was back ten minutes later, impressed by the size of his mother's cast, and the crutches lying next to her bed. She had already been sound asleep. "I turned off the TV, and left a light on for her. She's dead to the world. That's some cast."

"They said it was a nasty break. She's right. She's lucky it wasn't her hip. If you can call this luck. How was your day?"

"Only slightly better than hers. The press are driving us nuts on this case. You sound like shit. How do you feel?"

"Like I sound. I hope Charlie gets home in this weather. I'm really going to need his help this week."

Harry looked instantly apologetic. "I'm so

sorry I can't take a day off. I just can't right now."

"I know," she said mournfully. "Me too. I'm up to my ass in alligators at the office. Margaret took the week off. Her mother had a mastectomy."

"Jesus, is anyone around here still on their feet?"

"Thank God you are." They had chicken pox, broken ankles, colds. She just hoped Veronica stayed healthy, and Ginny got healthy, for the ball on Saturday. "If you want to sleep in Charlie's room tonight, it's okay. I don't want you to catch this cold or flu, or whatever it is. It's miserable."

"Don't be silly. I'm not afraid of you. I never get sick."

"Shhh!" she said, putting a finger to her lips. "Don't say that!" He laughed at her, took a shower, and was in bed with her half an hour later. She was still blowing and coughing, and had just checked on Max. He was sound asleep.

"It looks like you're going to be running an infirmary here this week," Harry said as he snuggled up next to her, and put his arms around her. She had her back to him, so she didn't breathe on him, and it was comforting feeling him next to her.

"I'm sorry about your mom. That was rotten luck for her."

"She's lucky to have you, Ollie . . . so am I . . . don't think I don't appreciate all you do for her. You're an amazing woman."

"Thank you," she said, as she drifted off to sleep in his arms. "You're not so bad yourself."

"I'll try and come home early tomorrow," he promised. She nodded, and within seconds, was fast asleep.

Chapter 6

Olympia got up at six the next morning to check on Frieda. Her cold was no better, but at least it wasn't worse. Her mother-in-law was still sound asleep, and there was no sign that she had gotten up during the night. She looked as though she hadn't moved an inch since Olympia had tucked her into bed the night before. Olympia had given her one of her own nightgowns, a big loose flannel one she'd worn when she was pregnant with Max. It was short on Frieda, and the sleeves were short, which she knew her mother-in-law didn't like. Her arms lay on top of the sheets, and Olympia could see the tattoo she always tried to hide. Seeing it, the rare times she did, never failed to make Olympia sad. It was impossible for her to imagine what those years must have been like for her. Knowing she had survived that always touched Olympia's heart. She tiptoed out of the room, and went back upstairs to take a shower. Harry was already nearly dressed. He had to be in the office for a press conference early that morning. And at seven, just as Olympia was combing her hair, Max woke up. He said he felt better, though he had as many spots as he'd had the night before, if not more.

"How are all your patients?" Harry asked as he put on his jacket and straightened his tie.

"Max says he feels better, and your mom is still asleep."

"Can you manage?" he asked, looking worried but also rushed.

Olympia laughed. "Do I have a choice?"

"I guess not," he said, looking apologetic. At least, he knew, now his mother going to the ball wouldn't be an issue. He had the excuse of staying home to take care of her, which he felt sure would get him off the hook, and make him look like less of a louse for not going. He had been feeling guilty about not going for weeks, but no matter how guilty he felt, he absolutely refused to go. And now his mother couldn't go, either. She could hardly go to a ball on crutches, unable to put any weight on one foot. He said nothing about it to his wife, but he was nonetheless relieved, although sorry about his mother's accident and the burden it would put on his wife. It seemed providential in some ways, for him.

"Don't worry," Olympia reassured him. "The sitter will be here in half an hour. She can take care of both of them. And Charlie will be home tonight. He can give us a hand till the girls come home. Then we can all take turns." He nodded, not entirely convinced that her optimism about her daughters was well founded. Ginny was not exactly famous for being helpful around the house. He knew Charlie would be a godsend, and if she was in the right mood and didn't have other plans, Veronica might lend a hand. Maybe. If there was no protest she felt she had to participate in, no one to picket, and no abused child or homeless person somewhere in the city whom she felt needed her help. Helping the family was low on her list of priorities, and as they all did, she counted on her mother to take care of everything. Somehow Olympia always did.

Harry felt guilty about that, too. Five minutes later, with a quick kiss to his wife, and a promise to be home as early as humanly possible, he left for work.

Olympia made Mickey Mouse pancakes for Max, put on a video for him, and checked on Frieda in the den again. She was still asleep when the sitter arrived. Olympia was grateful to see her, explained about the condition of both their patients, picked up her briefcase, and literally ran out the door. There was a foot of fresh snow on the ground, but it had finally stopped falling. And as usual, in weather like that, it took her half an hour to find a cab. Margaret called her in the office that afternoon, and asked how things were going. All Olympia could do was laugh.

"Well, let's see, Max has chicken pox, Frieda broke her ankle yesterday and is staying in our den. I have the cold of the century. Ginny is sick at school. And Charlie's coming home tonight, thank God."

"Other than that, Mrs. Lincoln, how was the performance?"

"Yeah. Right. When it rains, it pours. I just hope the girls stay in one piece till Saturday. After that, we can all fall apart."

"What's Harry doing to help?"

"Nothing at the moment. He's dealing with a crisis at the court of appeals."

"I know. I saw his press conference this morning. Just when I'd decided I hate the guy for not going to the ball with you, I fell in love with him all over again for the positions he takes. The guy is really a mensch, even though I think he's an asshole for not going with you on Saturday."

"You can't have everything, I guess," Olympia said with a sigh. "I love him, too. He stands for the right stuff, and is willing to fight for it to the death. Unfortunately, that includes his ideologies about the ball. I guess you can't have it both ways. He stands for what he believes. At least Chauncey is being decent. He must be sick."

"If he gives you a hard time on Saturday, I'll kick him in the shins."

"How's your mom doing?"

"Better than I thought she would. There is something about that generation of women. You've got to hand it to them. They're tough, and have a lot of guts. I'd be a mess. She's happy to be alive."

"Frieda's like that, too. All she could do

last night was apologize for being a burden on us. Once Max feels better and is no longer contagious, at least they can keep each other company. I think he's almost there now. I have to check. I don't want him giving her shingles."

"That's all you need." Margaret was impressed by all Olympia was handling. She always did. Kids, work, husband, crises. She somehow managed to juggle it all. It seemed to be the lot of working women. They had to be geniuses in the office, and tireless dynamos at home. As far as Margaret was concerned, it was too many hats to wear at once, which was why she had opted not to have kids. She could handle work and a husband, but four kids like Olympia's, or even one, would have been way more than she could cope with. As she pointed out regularly, she didn't even have pets or plants. Work was more than enough for her. And her husband was a dream. He took care of the house, organized their social life, and cooked for her when she got home. "Let me know if I can do anything to help," Margaret offered, but Olympia knew she had her hands full with her mother. She was just happy she'd be there Saturday night. With the girls nervous and wound up, Charlie and the other escort to keep track of, Frieda on crutches or in a wheelchair, and a potentially hostile ex-husband to deal with, Olympia was going to be crazed.

In spite of a new case that landed on her at four o'clock, Olympia left her office early, and managed to be home by five. Max was sitting on the couch in the den next to Frieda. She had her leg propped up on a chair, and Charlie was sitting with them, drinking tea, when Olympia walked in.

"Well, this looks like a cozy group. Hi, sweetheart," she said as she gave her son a big hug to welcome him home. She was visibly happy to have him back, and he looked equally pleased to see her. Max was still covered with calamine, but the doctor had assured them he was no longer contagious, so Frieda was enjoying his company, and had been all afternoon. Charlie had just gotten home, a few hours earlier than planned. "How's everybody feeling?" Olympia asked her patients.

"Better," Max said with a grin.

"Terrific," Frieda announced, looking at both her grandsons. "I was going to try and cook dinner for all of you, but Charlie won't let me." His mother looked at him with thanks and approval.

"I should hope not. We'll order Chinese. It's more fun." They sat chatting in the den for a while, and an hour later Harry came home. The day had gone well for him, and he was happy to see Charlie, too. The two went out to the kitchen to have a beer, while Olympia went upstairs to change into jeans. Max was happy where he was, with his grandma, watching TV. She was still apologizing for bothering them, but she was obviously enjoying being there with them.

Dinner was festive that night, and afterward everyone went to their own rooms, except Charlie, who hung out with his mother for a while. He looked like he had something on his mind, but when his mother asked him if that was the case, he insisted that he didn't. He just said he was happy to be home with them. He promised to keep Max and his grandmother company the next day, and a little while later he went out with friends. The weather had warmed up slightly that day, and what was left of the snow was turning to slush, and ice at night. Olympia warned him to be careful and remember what had happened to Frieda.

Charlie looked at her and smiled, and then left. Sometimes his mother still treated him like he was five.

Between running downstairs to check on Frieda, and putting Max to bed, cleaning up the kitchen, talking to Charlie, and taking a bath finally, Olympia didn't have time to talk to Harry alone until they were in bed that night.

"How did Charlie seem to you?" she asked, looking worried.

"Fine. Why? He seems to be having a great time playing hockey. And I think he's more relaxed about his future plans. He seemed uptight to me over Thanksgiving, but tonight I thought he was more laid-back."

"I can't put my finger on it. But I think something is still bothering him," she said with the finely tuned instincts of a mother.

"Did he say something to give you that impression?"

"No. He says he's fine. Maybe it's just my imagination, but I'm convinced something's on his mind."

"Stop looking for things to worry about," Harry chided her. "If he's upset, he'll tell you. Charlie's always good about that." Although he was private with others, he was exceptionally close to her.

"Maybe you're right," Olympia said, sounding unconvinced, and she mentioned it to Frieda the following day when she got home from work.

"It's funny you said that," Frieda said, looking pensive. "I can't tell you why, but I had the same impression when he sat here having tea with me yesterday. I can't tell if he's worried or sad. He seems preoccupied. Maybe he's worried about finding a job when he graduates," she said sensibly. He was a very responsible young man.

"He's seemed that way to me since that friend of his committed suicide last spring. I keep thinking it's that. I know he had counseling for it at school. Maybe it's something else. Or maybe it's nothing. Harry thinks I'm crazy," she said, sharing a cup of tea with her mother-in-law, which was the only peaceful moment she'd had all day. Frieda always told her she did too much. It was the fate of all working mothers, particularly those who made their living in the law, had a five-year-old at home, a husband, and three kids in college. It was a constant juggling act on the high wire, usually without a net, from morning till night.

"Men never see things like that," Frieda said, still thinking about Charlie. "It's probably nothing. He's probably just worried about what he'll do after graduation. It's a tough time for most kids. Like it or not, they have to leave the nest and grow up. He'll feel better once he makes his mind up about whether to take the job in California, find a job here, go to divinity school, or go to Oxford. They're all good choices to have, but until he makes a decision, he'll probably be a nervous wreck." They both agreed that he seemed troubled.

"I think you're right. I remember how scared I was when I left college. I had no family to fall back on. I was terrified, and then I married Chauncey, and I thought I was home free after that. As it turned out, not as home free as I thought."

"You were too young to get married," Frieda said with a frown, although she had been younger than that herself when she married Harry's father. But things were different then, they had been through the war, survived the horror of the camps, and had led a different life. During the war, people grew up fast, particularly as she had. Her youth had ended in the concentration camp at Dachau.

"At least I got three great kids out of it," Olympia said philosophically, and Frieda smiled in response.

"Yes, you did. Charlie's a wonderful boy, and the girls are terrific, too." And then she looked at her daughter-in-law with a determined expression. "I'm still going to the ball, you know. I don't care what you say, I wouldn't miss it for the world." Olympia was sorry Harry didn't feel the same way. "Harry said I should stay home with him. I'm still angry at him for not going, but that's his business if he wants to make a fool of himself with his stubborn ideas. I'm going. That's what I told him." There was a look of determination in her eyes.

Olympia looked at her and smiled. "I was going to try and talk you out of it. But I guess I don't have a chance of that."

"No, you don't," Frieda said, looking like an elderly lioness, as she sat on the couch with her leg in a cast, all propped up.

"Why don't I try and rent you a wheelchair?" Olympia said thoughtfully. "Charlie could pick it up tomorrow. That way you won't have to walk."

"It's embarrassing to go that way," the older woman admitted. "I hate to look like an invalid. But it makes sense. If you can get one, I'll go. And if you can't, I'll hobble in on crutches."

"You're a good sport," Olympia said with admiration. "And a wonderful grandmother." Frieda loved Olympia's older children just as much as she did Max, and made no difference between them.

"I'm going, if I have to go by ambulance and be carried in on a stretcher by paramedics. Besides, I want to wear my new dress. I've never been to a coming-out party, I'll probably never get another chance, and I'm not going to miss it." There were tears in her eyes as she said it. This was more than just a party for her. It was about being socially accepted in a way she never had been before. She had spent years of poverty, working in a sweatshop as a seamstress, beside her husband, to put their son through school. Just once before she died, she wanted to feel like Cinderella too, even if her son thought she was foolish. And she wanted to see her granddaughters make their debut. Olympia understood that, and vowed to make it happen for her. It was a dream come true for more than just the girls. It meant a lot to Frieda, too. More than Harry knew.

"We'll make it work, Frieda. I promise." The only thing Olympia couldn't figure out was who was going to push the wheelchair. She had to be at the hotel at five on Saturday to help the girls dress, and Charlie had to be there with them for rehearsal. There was no one to wheel her into the hotel, except Harry, who refused to go. She was thinking of asking Margaret and her husband to pick her up, if Olympia rented them all a limo. It was the only way to do it.

Olympia asked Harry about the ball cautiously again that night after dinner, and reminded him that with his mother disabled, the logistics of getting her there were going to be a lot harder than they would have been otherwise. She needed someone to help her, and was hoping he'd volunteer so she didn't have to ask him directly.

"I already told her she shouldn't go," he said, looking annoyed.

"She wants to," Olympia said calmly,

without going into the many reasons she thought it was important to Frieda.

"She's just being stubborn," he said bluntly.

"So are you." There was an edge to her voice that hadn't been there before. He was absolutely refusing to help her, and it was beginning to seriously irk her. The least he could do was help his mother get there, since she wanted to so badly. "This means a lot to your mother. Maybe more than just the obvious." In Chauncey's case, it was about rank snobbism. But Frieda had worked hard all her life, sacrificed much, survived persecution, and come through a long, difficult history to get here. If she wanted to go to a debutante cotillion, for whatever reason, Olympia thought she had a right to; and she was going to do everything she could to support it. Besides, the twins adored their grandmother and wanted her there. She deserved this one special night as much as the girls. It was her night, too. Olympia understood that. Harry didn't. He refused to. His own political point of view was more important to him than the dreams of a young girl, or an old woman. "I think this is really important to her," Olympia said gently.

"It shouldn't be," he said firmly. "And even if it is, I am a judge of the court of appeals. I can't endorse a discriminatory event just to please my mother, or my wife, or your daughters. I'm tired of being made to feel like an asshole about it, Ollie. I firmly believe in what I'm doing. I can't be there."

"I'm sure you wouldn't be the first Jew who has been a guest at The Arches. For all I know, there are even Jewish girls who've come out there."

"I doubt it. And even if that's true, I still have to take a position on this and stick to it. I don't think Martin Luther King ever went to a ball hosted by the Ku Klux Klan."

"Do you and Veronica have to boycott everything you don't believe in? I can't even buy groceries when she's home, without worrying about who I'm offending or persecuting. If I buy grapes, it's an affront to Cesar Chavez. If I buy South African goods, I'm disrespecting Nelson Mandela. Hell, half the time if I put on a sweater or a pair of shoes, or eat a piece of fruit in my own kitchen, I'm pissing someone off. It sure makes life complicated, and in this case, I think our family is more important than your goddamn political views. All your mother wants now is to go to a party to watch her stepgranddaughters make their debut, which I'll admit is an archaic tradition, but that's all it is. It's a party, one night in a girl's life that makes her feel special, like a bat mitzvah. You can't suck it up for one night?" She was obviously slowly getting angry about his position, but Harry only looked at her and shook his head. He had heard her and knew it was important to her, and his mother. But he disagreed with them, and wouldn't budge an inch.

"No, I can't."

"Fine." She spat the word at him with her eyes blazing. "Then to hell with you, if your principles and political views mean more to you than we do. I think this time you're really missing the point."

"I know you feel that way," he said quietly, looking profoundly unhappy. "Principles aren't like a hat you take on and off when it suits you. They're a crown of thorns that you have an obligation to wear no matter what."

Olympia didn't say another word, and left the room before she got really angry at him, and said something she'd regret. She knew there was going to be no compromise on this one. Harry was truly adamant, and she had lost the war. Like it or not, and fair or not, she was going to be the one who had to suck it up.

Chapter 7

Once the girls came home from college, everything in the house was chaos. Their friends came and went, the phone rang constantly. Other girls who were making their debut at The Arches showed up to talk to Ginny, giggle, squeal, and take a peek at her dress. All the girls approved when they saw it. They all agreed it was gorgeous. Veronica holed up in her own room with her friends, none of whom were planning to come out.

Frieda left the door to the den open, and enjoyed watching the arrivals and departures. Olympia was bringing in kosher food for her, and Charlie helped her pick it up, and serve it to Frieda on separate dishes on trays. She had been extremely reasonable about not being quite as rigid about it as normal. She knew how complicated it was for Olympia to worry about that, too. And she was sure God would forgive her as long as she didn't eat cream sauces on her meat, or eat lobster or shrimp. Olympia was fastidious and mindful of what she served. And as predicted, Charlie was a godsend for her. He helped her with whatever he could.

On Thursday night, they celebrated Chanukah. Olympia lit the candles, as Frieda said the prayers with her. They exchanged gifts, as they would every night for eight days. Olympia was happy to have Frieda staying at the house with them. It made the whole family seem closer. And the religious holiday provided a sane distraction from the ball, at least for one night.

Ginny was excited that Steve was coming to town on Friday night, and Veronica continued to promise her mother that Jeff was totally suitable and wouldn't spike his hair. He wasn't due to arrive until Saturday morning, which seemed tight to Olympia, but he had something to do in Providence on Friday night, and Veronica said it was the best he could do. There was no point arguing with her. With the coming-out ball only days away, she was in a rotten mood.

It occurred to Olympia late Thursday night that although Veronica swore she had them, she had never seen her white satin evening shoes. She decided to check in her closet to make sure that they were in fact there. If not, she'd have to buy her a pair. Or Veronica was likely to do something crazy, like wear sneakers or red shoes. She let herself into the room as Veronica came out of the shower towel-drying her hair with her back to her mother. Olympia stopped in her tracks and stared at her in horror. Right in the center of her back was a giant tattoo. It was a huge multicolored butterfly with a wingspread the size of a dinner plate. Without even realizing it, Olympia screamed, and Veronica jumped about a foot, and wheeled around. She hadn't heard her mother come in.

"Oh my God! *What is that?*" She knew perfectly well what it was. She just couldn't believe that Veronica had done that to herself. It was huge. Olympia burst into tears.

"Come on, Mom . . . please . . . I'm sorry . . . I was going to tell you about it . . . I've always wanted to do it . . . I love it . . . you'll get used to it. . . ." Veronica looked panicked. The one thing her mother had always forbidden them was piercings or tattoos. She had let them pierce their ears, but anywhere else was taboo. And tattoos were beyond the pale.

"I can't believe you did that!" Olympia said, sitting on the edge of Veronica's bed. She was feeling faint. Her baby's body had been desecrated. She couldn't even imagine Veronica living with that for the rest of her life. It was obscene. She wanted her to have it removed, but she knew that if she suggested it, her daughter would refuse. "You look like you just got out of prison."

"Everyone has them at school. I'm eighteen, Mom. I have a right to do what I want with my own body."

"Do you have any idea what that looks like, or what it will look like when you're fifty? Are you nuts?" And then she looked utterly panicked. "Did Ginny get one, too?" Veronica looked embarrassed as she sat down on the bed next to her mother and put her arms around her.

"I'm sorry, Mom. I didn't mean to upset you. I've wanted one for years." Olympia knew that was true, but she thought she had convinced her otherwise. It never occurred to her that Veronica would defy her and get a tattoo the minute she went away to school.

"Why couldn't you get one on your bottom, where no one would see it? Do you have any idea how that looks?"

"Mom, I love it . . . honestly . . . it's me . . ."

And then Olympia had another thought. Veronica's debut dress was backless and plunged nearly to her waist. "We have to get you a new dress."

"No, we don't," Veronica said calmly. "I like the one I have." It was the first time she had admitted that, but there was no way Olympia would let her wear that dress now and show off her tattoo. She'd die first.

"I'm not letting you come out at The Arches with that *thing* on your back." Ginny walked into the room as she said it, looking for a can of hairspray, saw her mother's devastated expression, and then looked at her twin.

Veronica spoke first. "Mom knows." Ginny looked uncomfortable to be caught between the two, and started to leave the room.

"You stay right here. If either of you ever

gets another one, I'm killing you both. And that goes for Charlie, too."

"He'd never do it," Veronica reassured her. "He's too afraid to piss you off. So is Ginny."

"What makes you so brave?" Olympia asked miserably, blowing her nose in a tissue. She felt as though someone had died, although she knew it was only a tattoo.

"I figured you'd forgive me," Veronica said with a sheepish smile, and hugged her again, as her mother wiped her eyes.

"Don't be so sure. And we have to do something about the dress. I came in here to look for your shoes." They had shared such a wonderful Chanukah only hours before, and now there was this, to spoil it all for her.

"I can't find my shoes," Veronica admitted blithely. "I think I gave them away."

"Great." It was nothing now compared to what she had done to her body. "I'll get you a pair tomorrow." She was taking the day off, as she always did on Friday. She had a million things to do. She still had to get a wheelchair for Frieda from a medical supply store. She had to pick Frieda's dress up at her apartment, and now get Veronica a pair of shoes. But all she could think of as she sat there was the butterfly tattoo. "How am I supposed to find you a dress in one day?"

"I'll wear a sweater over it," Veronica volunteered as Olympia started to cry again. This was too much for her already frayed nerves. Frieda's accident, Max's chicken pox, Harry's stubbornness, the cold she had had all week, and now the horror of the tattoo.

"You can't wear a sweater over an evening dress. Maybe I can find you a white satin stole somewhere. If I can't, we're screwed."

"Come on, Mom, no one's going to get upset about it."

"The hell they're not, and I already am. You can at least indulge me, for chrissake," Olympia said, heartbroken and furious all at the same time.

"I am," Veronica reminded her. "I'm coming out, aren't I? You know I didn't want to. So give me a break."

"I am. I just didn't know you'd break my heart in exchange. Was this your revenge for making you come out? The iron butterfly?"

"No, Mom," Veronica said, looking unhappy. "I got it the first week of school, as a symbol of my independence and flying free. My metamorphosis into being an adult."

"Wonderful. I guess I'm lucky you didn't put a caterpillar on there too, to show the before and after." She stood up then and looked at both her daughters, and without another word, she left the room. She passed Harry on the stairs and didn't say a word to him. She went downstairs to the kitchen and made herself a cup of tea. He could see how upset she was, and thought it was still about him. It was after midnight, and Olympia was obviously severely overwrought.

Frieda saw her walk past her open door with her head down, and a few minutes later hobbled into the kitchen on her crutches. Olympia was sitting at the kitchen table, crying over her cup of tea. She was thinking about the backless dress and what they were going to do. More than that, she was thinking about Veronica's perfect young body, and how she had defaced it. It would never be the same.

"Uh-oh," Frieda said, looking at her. She'd had a feeling something was wrong, which was why she had come in. It wasn't like Olympia not to stick her head in the door to see how she was. "What's wrong?" she asked, as she gingerly let herself down into a kitchen chair across the table from her daughter-in-law. "Nothing serious, I hope," Frieda said, looking worried. She hoped Harry wasn't being difficult again. She knew he had added to Olympia's stresses all week by refusing to attend the ball with her. She had never before seen her daughter-in-law in tears, and it upset her severely. The evening had seemed perfect until then, and now the mood was shattered.

"I was going to stop by and say good-bye before I committed suicide, but I thought I'd have a cup of tea first." She smiled at her mother-in-law through her tears.

"That bad? Who did this to you? I'll beat them up for you, just tell me who it is." It was like having a mom again, and it touched Olympia to the core, as she reached out for Frieda's hand across the table. Veronica's tattoo had just been too much for her. It seemed silly, but she was devastated over it. It was such a stupid thing to do. And worse yet, it was permanent. Olympia was sure Veronica would regret it in years to come, but she'd have to live with it anyway. And it was complicated having it removed, even if she wanted to one day. "If Harry made you cry like this, I'll kill him," Frieda said with a stern air as Olympia shook her head.

"Veronica," she said, and then blew her nose. It was bright red from blowing it all week. At least the antibiotics had helped Ginny. She was much better by the time she got home. Olympia could hardly say the words as she looked across the table at her mother-in-law. "She got a tattoo."

"A tattoo?" Frieda looked stunned. It hadn't even occurred to her. On a list of possible tragedies, it would have been last on her list. "Where?"

"In the middle of her back," Olympia said miserably. "This big!" She framed her hands to indicate the size of it all too accurately.

"Oh dear," Frieda said, digesting the information Olympia had shared with her. "That's not good. What a foolish thing to do. I know they're fashionable now, but she'll be sorry she did it one day."

"She's thrilled with it," Olympia said unhappily. "I have to get her a new dress tomorrow. She can't wear the one she has. I have to get her one now with a high back. Or a stole. I'm not sure what kind of miracle

I can pull off in a day." And she was still feeling sick.

Frieda looked thoughtful for a moment, and nodded. "Get me four yards of white satin tomorrow, good stuff, not the cheesy synthetics. I'll make a stole for her. She can wear it for the presentation at least. After that, well . . . after that it's up to her and you. Would she wear a stole?" Frieda looked as worried as Olympia, not only for the long term, but for the debut ball, which was only two days away.

"She'll wear a suit of armor now if I tell her to," Olympia said quietly. "I don't know when she was planning to tell me about it, but I'd have had a heart attack if I'd seen it when she makes her bow." Olympia shook her head and looked at her mother-in-law. The two women exchanged a smile across the table. "Kids. They sure keep life exciting, don't they?" Olympia laughed ruefully, and her mother-in-law patted her hand.

"It keeps you young. Believe me, once they stop surprising us, it's all over and you miss them like crazy. My life has never been the same since Harry went to college and left home."

"At least he never got a tattoo."

"No, but he got drunk with his friends and tried to enlist in the Marines at seventeen. Thank God they rejected him because he'd had asthma all his life. If they'd have taken him then, it would have killed me. His father almost killed him. All right, let's be practical. Tomorrow you have to get me four yards of white satin, and we'll make her a stole to cover the tattoo. It's easier than finding a new dress, and I can have it done in a few hours. I don't even need my sewing machine. I can do it by hand."

"I love you, Frieda. I swear, I thought I was going to faint when I saw that thing on her back. She had just gotten out of the shower. I guess she's been hiding it for months."

"It could be worse. It could be a skull and crossbones, or some boy's name she won't remember by next year. How's Ginny's romance, by the way? Is the boy still coming?"

"Tomorrow night apparently, and she says it's okay. Veronica doesn't like him, and she has pretty good judgment about men, better than Ginny. I hope he's a nice kid. She's all excited about his seeing her in her gown."

"It's all so sweet," Frieda said, looking

starry-eyed, "and don't worry, we'll cover the tattoo. No one will know except us." It was lovely having a mother-in-law who wanted to solve problems and not cause them. Olympia knew that was rare and appreciated her enormously. She was more like her own mother than Harry's.

Olympia told Harry about the tattoo when she went to bed, and he was as upset as she was. Defacing one's body was not only against his aesthetic principles, but also against his religion. He could just imagine how Olympia felt. She was still upset about it early the next morning when she went out to buy the white satin. Afterward, she went to Manolo Blahnik to buy the white satin shoes, and had the fabric in Frieda's hands by noon. It was exactly the same tone, brightness, and weight as the fabric in the dress. It was perfect. By four that afternoon, when Charlie and Olympia came back from picking up the wheelchair, Frieda had the exquisitely sewn handmade stole hanging pristinely on a hanger. It was all done, and when Veronica modeled it for them when she got home, it was exactly the right length, and she promised to wear it the following night. For the ball at least, problem solved. It was a load off Olympia's mind, if not her heart.

She, Harry, and his mother were planning a quiet dinner at home that night. Harry offered to cook. Max was still in bed, watching videos night and day. And the older three were going out. Olympia was looking forward to a peaceful evening. Frieda tried the wheelchair, and declared it comfortable and efficient. It was going to make her life much easier the following evening. They left it folded up in the hall, so the driver could put it in the limo. Margaret had agreed to come by and pick Frieda up, since Olympia would already be at the hotel with the girls.

They enjoyed a cozy dinner that night on the second night of Chanukah. Frieda lit the candles and said the traditional prayer. Olympia loved to hear her do it, and it reminded Harry of his childhood, although he loved it when Olympia did it, too.

They were all getting ready to go to bed, when Olympia heard Ginny come in. There were voices in the downstairs hall, outside Frieda's room, the sound of running on the stairs, and then Olympia saw her fly past her open door and heard her sobbing.

"Uh-oh." She looked at Harry. "Trouble in

River City. I'll be back." She went down the hall to Ginny's room and found her lying on the bed, crying uncontrollably. It took her mother nearly ten minutes to find out what was wrong. Steve had arrived from Providence that night, gone to dinner with her, and told her that he had actually come to New York to tell her it was over. He dumped her, and already had another girlfriend. Ginny was beside herself. She was crazy about him. Olympia couldn't help wondering why he had come to New York to deliver the message in person the night before her big event. He couldn't tell her afterward, or even on the phone? It seemed like a nasty stunt to her, and a devastating one to Ginny. There was little she could say to console her.

"I'm sorry, sweetheart . . . I'm so sorry . . . it was a rotten thing to do. . . ." It didn't seem fair to tell her she'd forget about him and there would be another thousand men in her life, after him. Right now it felt like a mortal blow, and a cruel trick.

"I'm not going tomorrow . . . ," Ginny said in muffled tones into the mattress. "I can't. . . . I don't care anymore. . . . I'm not going to come out. . . . I wish I were dead. . . ."

"No, you don't. And you have to come out. This is a special moment in your life. You've been looking forward to it. You can't let this guy spoil it for you. Don't give him that. I know it feels awful right now, but you'll feel better tomorrow night . . . honest . . . I know you will." Her heart was sinking. Why did he have to do that to her now? Couldn't he have waited till Sunday? Didn't the bastard have a conscience? Apparently not. Olympia went on talking to her for an hour, at the end of which Ginny still insisted she wouldn't do it. She was going to stay home the following night with Max and Harry. Veronica would have to come out alone. "I'm not going to let you do that," Olympia said firmly. "I know you feel awful right now. But tomorrow night you're going to look beautiful on Charlie's arm, you're going to make your bow, and every boy in the room will fall in love with you. Ginny, you have to do this."

"I can't, Mom," she said, staring up at the ceiling, and looking as though the world had come to an end, as tears continued to roll down her cheeks. Olympia knew it felt awful, but there was no doubt in her mind that there would be life after Steve, the little shit. She wanted to strangle him for inflicting so much pain on her baby. All she could do now was help pick up the pieces.

It was nearly midnight when she got back to her own room. Ginny was miserable but calm again. She had finally stopped crying. And Harry was sound asleep. Olympia lay in bed next to him, closed her eyes, and silently prayed. . . . Please God, let everyone stay sane tomorrow and behave decently tomorrow night. . . . I can't take any more surprises. . . . Please God, just for one night. . . . Thank you, God. . . . Goodnight. And with that, she fell asleep.

Chapter 8

The next day, Saturday, the day of the ball, dawned icy cold and brilliantly sunny. It didn't snow, it didn't rain, it was colder than the north pole, but it was a gorgeous day when Olympia woke up with trepidation. All she wanted to do was get through the day, dress the girls, watch them curtsy and come down the stairs, and survive the evening. It didn't seem like a lot to ask, but these days it was beginning to seem like a miracle if no one broke a leg, came down with a rare disease, or had a nervous breakdown. If anyone had one of those, Olympia was planning to be first.

At noon, she had to take the girls to get their hair done. She had an appointment in the same salon at two herself. By four they'd all be finished. She made breakfast for everyone, brought Frieda hers on a tray, and Frieda wished her luck for that night. She asked if there was anything she could do to help, but as far as Olympia knew, everything was in order. Both girls were still asleep. Harry had gone out early to play squash at his club. Max was feeling better. Charlie had spent the night with friends. For the moment, the house was peaceful.

At eleven o'clock, Ginny woke up and came rushing downstairs with a look of panic. She found her mother in Frieda's room, exploded into the room, and announced, "I lost a glove!" One of the long white ones, presumably, that were mandatory to wear. Her mother looked calm.

"No, you didn't. I saw them both yesterday. They were on top of your dresser, with your bag."

Ginny looked instantly uncomfortable and slightly guilty. "I took them to Debbie's last night, to show her how gorgeous they were, and then everything happened with Steve. I forgot one of them there. She said the dog chewed it to bits last night."

"Oh for God's sake . . ." Olympia struggled not to get upset. "When am I supposed to get another pair? . . . All right, all right . . . I'll go, now before I take you to the hairdresser. I hope they have another pair in your size." Frieda watched with enormous admiration as Olympia handled the situation with aplomb. Ten minutes later Olympia was wearing jeans, a ski parka, fur-lined boots, and rushing out of the house. Miraculously, she was back just before noon, with another pair of the required gloves in Ginny's size. Problem solved. Disaster averted. Round one.

They left for the hairdresser at five to twelve, and after she dropped them off, Olympia came back to the house. She fed Max, made Frieda a kosher meal, and had a sandwich waiting for Harry when he came back from playing squash. Ten minutes later Charlie got home, and hovered around his mother. He seemed nervous, and she wondered if he was anxious about that night. She assured him he would be fine. She sat at the table for half an hour with Harry, and they chatted about assorted things. She didn't mention the ball to him. The subject was closed, and would stay that way. She went upstairs to change, and Charlie wandered into her bedroom.

"Are you okay?" she asked, and he nodded, looking distracted. "Something on your mind?" He shook his head and left again. She started to worry about him, but didn't have time. Then Margaret called. Her mother was running a fever after her mastectomy, and might have an infection. Margaret was still coming to the ball that night, but she was going to be late. She had to stay with her mother at the hospital and help her eat dinner. She didn't have time to pick Frieda up. She felt terrible to let Ollie down, but she had no other choice. Her mother was feeling rotten. Olympia said she understood, and stood staring at the phone for a minute, trying to figure it out. She had to be at the hotel with the girls from five o'clock on. Charlie had to be there by four, which left no one to accompany Frieda in the limousine. She had an idea then, and went to discuss it with Harry.

He listened carefully, convinced she was going to try and manipulate him into going with her at the last minute. She had given up all hope of that. All she wanted from him was to get his mother into the limousine, put the wheelchair in with her, and call Olympia on her cell phone the minute they left the house. Olympia would then go down to the lobby and out to the street, meet Frieda in the limousine, put her in the wheelchair, and get her upstairs to dinner before the ball. Olympia made it sound easy. The fact that she'd be dressing two hysterical girls, watching them be photographed, and trying to calm them down, while dressing herself, she didn't mention to her husband.

"Can you do that for me?" she asked after outlining her plan for his mother.

"Of course I can. She's my mother." Olympia made no comment about his not going with them, nor asked him to join her. All she wanted was for him to get his mother into the limousine and call her. They both knew anyone could do that, and it was the least he could do, whatever his political opinions. He looked slightly embarrassed as he assured his wife he'd take care of it on his end.

"Great. Thanks. 'Bye," she said, and flew out of the house to get her hair done. Ginny's was done by then. Veronica was getting hers done at the same time as her mother. Ginny got her nails done while they had their hair done. Veronica had had her nails done first. It was orchestrated like the landing of the Allied troops in Normandy on D-day.

At three-thirty Olympia called the house to remind Charlie to leave for the hotel, with his tailcoat, trousers, shirt, white tie, vest, socks, and patent-leather shoes. And the gloves he had to wear. He said he would leave in five minutes. He was ready to go.

Olympia and the girls got home at four-fifteen, perfectly coiffed and beautifully manicured. Harry was playing cards with Max. Charlie had left. And Frieda was having a nap. They gathered up their things, and mother and daughters left for the hotel in good order at four-thirty. They checked into the room Olympia had reserved for them at the hotel where the ball was held. Olympia took a minute to call Harry then. She had scarcely said good-bye to him when she left. She reminded him of what time to put his mother in the limo, and to call her on her cell phone. He said he understood, and sounded very quiet. He promised to wake his mother at six o'clock, and would help her dress. The limousine was coming for her at seven-fifteen. There was a dinner for the girls, their escorts, and their families. The rest of the guests were coming at nine. Rehearsal was at five. It was in the same ballroom as the ball was held. Olympia got the girls downstairs on schedule, at ten to five.

As it so happened, Veronica's escort, Jeff Adams, was walking in, with his tailcoat on a hanger, just as Olympia and the girls appeared at the entrance to the ballroom for rehearsal. Olympia closed her eyes, hoping she was hallucinating. As it turned out, she wasn't. Jeff Adams had bright blue hair. Not dark blue, or midnight blue, which might be mistaken for black in a darkened ballroom. It was somewhere between turquoise and sapphire, and there was no mistaking what color it was, in any light. He looked extremely pleased with himself, and insufferably arrogant as he shook Olympia's hand. Veronica looked at him and laughed. Ginny still looked like a zombie, after Steve's perfidy of the night before. He had told her that even though he was dumping her for another girl, he was "willing" to come to the ball. And much to Olympia's horror, Ginny had told him he could. She said she wanted one last night with him. Thinking about it made Olympia feel sick, but she didn't want to upset Ginny more. He was due to show up at nine with the other guests, since he wasn't her escort. He was going to sit at Olympia's table with their other guests. Olympia was sorely tempted to stab him with a fork. She would have liked the same fate for Jeff, as Veronica congratulated him on the fabulous color of his hair. He handed his tailcoat to Olympia, and asked her to hang on to it for him during rehearsal. She wanted to kill him.

They lined up for rehearsal in four straight lines, two of debutantes, and two of escorts, while members of the ball committee walked between them and inspected them. A somber-looking matron in black slacks and a Chanel jacket stopped directly in front of Jeff, and explained the situation to him in no uncertain terms. After rehearsal he had until nine o'clock that night to return his hair to a normal, human color, whichever one he preferred, whether his own or not, or if he preferred not to change his hair color, Veronica would be provided with another escort for the ball. The head of the committee made it clear to him that it was entirely his choice. He looked somewhat subdued, while Veronica continued to laugh at him. She seemed to find the entire escapade hysterically funny, and her mother was seriously upset at her. Between the recent discovery of the tattoo on her back, and the color of her escort's hair, she seemed to be entering a new phase of her life. It was no longer enough to throw out the grapes her mother bought, now apparently she had to shock everyone and make a spectacle of herself. Olympia was far from pleased.

She mentioned it to her when they went back to their room after rehearsal, to dress.

"Veronica, that wasn't funny. All he did was make the members of the committee mad at him, and you by association."

"Come on, Mom, don't be so uptight. If we have to do something as dumb as this, we might as well have a sense of humor about it."

"It wasn't humorous," Olympia insisted. "It was rude and annoying. Is he going to dye it back?"

"Of course he is. He just did it to be funny."

"He wasn't." Olympia looked seriously aggravated, and by then, Ginny was crying again. She had just heard from Steve on her cell phone. He was no longer sure he was coming. He thought it might be too hard for her. Ginny told him between sobs that it would be harder if he didn't. She damn near begged him, while Olympia cringed listening to her, and finally he agreed to come. If Olympia's thoughts of him could have killed him, the infamous Steve would have been dead on the spot. Instead, he was going to be her dinner guest, and break her daughter's heart on one of the most important nights of her life.

At six o'clock the girls put on their dresses, and Olympia stood looking at them with tears in her eyes. The moment was unforgettable. They looked like fairy princesses, and Veronica's stole demurely covered her back.

At seven they met with the photographer, while their mother stayed upstairs to get dressed. Her pantyhose ran the moment she put them on, but fortunately she'd brought a spare pair. Her zipper caught when she put on her dress, but she managed to salvage it somehow. She stopped for a minute, tried to slow down, and caught her breath. Her hair looked fine. She had put her makeup on, and it looked decent with her dress. Her shoes were killing her, but she expected that. Her evening bag was perfect. She put on the pearls that had been her mother's, and the earrings that matched. She looked in the mirror, and everything seemed all right to her. She put lipstick on, put on the matching navy blue stole, just as her cell phone rang. Harry said he had put his mother in the limousine. It was seven-fifteen. And he said Max was feeling better.

"I'll go right down and pick your mother up," Olympia said, sounding out of breath.

"How's it going?" he asked, seeming concerned. Olympia was obviously a nervous wreck, he could hear it in her voice.

"I don't know. I think I'm more nervous than the girls. They both look gorgeous. They're having photographs taken right now. I have to join them as soon as your mother comes. Chauncey and Felicia are probably already downstairs." She wasn't looking forward to that.

She didn't tell Harry that she missed him, because she didn't want to make him feel guiltier than she already had. There was no point. It hadn't gotten her anywhere. She had a brief fantasy that he was in the limousine with her mother-in-law, but she could hear from the sound of Max talking in the background that Harry was obviously still at home. This was just going to be one of those disappointments that happened in a marriage, that she would have to swallow and forget. There were lots of other things he did right. And other than this, he had always been there for her, and would be again. This was one thing he couldn't do for her, and that she had no choice but to accept. There was no point damaging their relationship over a coming-out ball he wouldn't attend. She couldn't allow it to mean that much. She said good-bye to him hurriedly, left the room, and took the elevator downstairs. She was waiting on the street for Frieda, shivering, when her limousine arrived. Frieda looked like a dignified grande dame in her elegant black dress, with her hair swept into a smooth French twist she had done herself, as the doorman helped her into the wheelchair, and wheeled her inside. Olympia took over from there.

Olympia got her in the elevator, and up to the ballroom level, where the girls' families were gathering to be photographed, looking proud. The mothers were given corsages of gardenias to pin on their dresses, carry, or wear on their wrists, and the girls were given wreaths of tiny white flowers to wear on their heads, and bouquets to carry when they walked out onstage. There was something exquisitely virginal about fifty young women all dressed in white, with wreaths of flowers on their heads, carrying their bouquets. It brought tears to Olympia's and Frieda's eyes.

"They look so beautiful," Frieda whispered to her, and Olympia was profoundly touched to see what it meant to her. She was the grandmother of their hearts. She looked at Olympia then and shook her head. "I'm so sorry Harry's not here with you. He's even more stubborn than his father. I told him tonight I was ashamed of him," she said unhappily, and Olympia patted her arm.

"It's all right." There was nothing else she could say. He had taken a position, and stuck by it, whether she was disappointed or not. Frieda was stunned by her daughter-in-law's generosity about it. She wasn't sure she would have been capable of it herself. She was furious with her son, for letting Olympia down. But before she could say more about it, a tall blond man in white tie and tails approached them, with an equally tall blond woman at his side. It was Chauncey and Felicia. Olympia introduced them to Frieda. Felicia said good evening to Frieda politely, Chauncey ignored her entirely while he greeted his ex-wife. In spite of the fact that she'd dressed quickly, and paid little attention to herself, Olympia looked spectacular that night. Chauncey looked her over with a practiced air.

"You're looking well, Olympia," he said, kissing her cheek. She thanked him, and shook hands with Felicia, who looked silly in a pink satin dress that was way too low and way too tight. Olympia was startled to notice that she looked cheap. She didn't remember her looking that way, but it had been years since they last met. She hadn't improved with age. And she could see that the girls' unflattering comments about her were right. She looked foolish, and dressed inappropriately for her age. Olympia's well-cut navy blue satin evening gown looked more elegant, much sexier, and wasn't nearly as low cut. Olympia looked spectacular and dignified. Chauncey seemed to notice it, too. He put an arm around her shoulders, and gave her a hug "for old times' sake." Looking at him, Olympia suspected he was already drunk. And Felicia was well on her way. This was not going to be fun.

"Where are our girls?" he asked, glancing around.

"They're having photographs taken with their escorts. They'll take some with us in a few minutes." She felt like a tour director on board the ship to hell. Everything about the evening had become difficult, from Ginny's heartbreak to Veronica's escort's blue hair, not to mention the butterfly tattoo, or the events of the week, from broken ankles to chicken pox, cold, and flu. It had been an insanely stressful week, and standing there with Chauncey and his wife, Olympia found it impossible to relax. It would have been easier for her if Harry were there. Instead, she was pushing his mother in a wheelchair. She could no longer remember what stroke of insanity had made her think this would be fun. So far, it had been anything but. She just hoped Ginny didn't lose another glove.

She got her first glimpse of Jeff then, since their encounter that afternoon. He walked out of the ballroom with Veronica, and his hair was no longer sapphire blue, but an inky dense shoe polish black. Not exactly a natural color, and it was easy to see it had been dyed. It looked very punk rock, but the committee had decided to ignore it. Olympia was grateful for small mercies. Jeff glanced at her with a look of supercilious amusement, and she had a powerful urge to slap him. He was arrogance personified, although admittedly a handsome kid, but the kind of boy who thought he was smarter than everyone, especially anyone's parents. She couldn't help wondering if Veronica had invited him to upset her. She had done everything else possible to do so since Olympia and Chauncey had forced her to make her debut. Veronica was doing it, but no one was going to force her to take it seriously, or enjoy it. And Ginny was still looking upset when both girls kissed their father, and said hello to Felicia. She told the girls they looked beautiful, and Frieda cried when she hugged them.

After family photographs, the girls, their escorts, and the girls' families all went to another floor for dinner. Olympia was sitting between Veronica and Frieda. Chauncey and Felicia were next to Ginny. Everything seemed to be going perfectly, until Chauncey got up to go to the men's room, halfway through dinner. Veronica had draped her stole over the back of her chair. It was too awkward to manage during dinner, in the slippery satin. She and her mother had momentarily forgotten why she had worn it in the first place. Chauncey stopped directly behind her chair and looked as if he'd been shot. He turned directly toward his ex-wife and stared at her in disbelief.

"Are you out of your mind?" She had no idea what had set him off, except that she'd noticed he'd been drinking. Felicia looked just as mystified as she did, and then Olympia saw him look at the artwork on his daughter's back. "Are you both totally crazy? How could you let this happen?" He was looking over his daughter's head right at Olympia.

"Actually, Chauncey," she said, looking annoyed but aloof, "she got out of her cell and escaped, despite the handcuffs. Almost like Houdini."

"You're not amusing. That's the most disgusting thing I've ever seen. She'll have it surgically removed, or I'm not paying tuition." Whether or not he paid tuition for them seemed to have become his only form of blackmail and control over her, and recently, his mantra.

"I don't think this is the place to discuss that," Olympia said with a quelling look.

Everyone at the table was watching, and no one had seen what he was talking about, since the others were facing Veronica across the table. She turned to look at him, with open outrage.

"Stop threatening my mother. I'm eighteen years old, and I wanted to do it. She didn't even know I did it till this week."

"Veronica, you're out of control," he said in booming tones, which the entire room could hear. "If you're going to disfigure yourself in that way, you belong in prison, with other people who look like you." Olympia was momentarily terrified that Veronica would tell him to go fuck himself, and cause a bigger scene than they already had. Everyone was riveted by the scene. He wasn't subtle, and thanks to the booze he'd already consumed, he was loud. Even Felicia looked surprised by the fuss he was making.

"I'm not going to discuss this with you, Dad. Why don't you grow up?" Veronica said, standing up and looking him in the eye. "It's a tattoo, not a crime. Why don't you have another drink? I'm sure that will make you feel better," she said in icy tones, and then walked out of the room. Jeff saw her leave, and followed her out. As she disappeared, everyone at the table got a full view of the tattoo Chauncey was objecting to so loudly. Felicia turned to look and gasped. She assured everyone at the table that none of her own daughters would think of doing a thing like that, and then admitted that her oldest daughter was just thirteen. Olympia knew that a lot was due to change in Felicia's life in the next five years. In spite of one's best efforts, there was only so much one could do to control one's kids.

Olympia didn't like it either, but much to her surprise, she thought Veronica had handled the scene with dignity and decorum, far more so than her father. Charlie glanced down the table at his mother, and a moment later, the conversations around them resumed. It wasn't until after dinner that one of the other mothers came over to talk to Olympia, with a look of sympathetic amusement.

"I know how you feel. My nineteen-year-old came home from UC Santa Cruz with tattooed sleeves. They're the worst thing I've ever seen, but there wasn't a damn thing I could do about it. I don't even want to think what that will look like when her arms start sagging. There are worse things they could be doing." Olympia wasn't sure what those would be, but she was sure she could come up with something, if she thought about it. And she was grateful for the other mother's compassionate reassurance.

"I'm still in shock. I only saw it two days ago for the first time. My mother-in-law made her a stole to go with her dress tonight. I wasn't sure the committee would appreciate the artwork."

"I'm sure she's not the first girl who's come out with a tattoo. My older daughter's escort showed up with a bull ring in his nose."

"One of ours showed up tonight with blue hair," Olympia admitted, and both women laughed at the foibles of youth.

"Things are a lot different than they were in our day. My grandmother had a fit when I wore a strapless gown. I think in her day everyone had to wear little cap sleeves to cover their arms. It's just the way things are today."

"I guess you're right," Olympia said, finally calming down. She could see that Chauncey was still fuming when he resumed his seat. He glared across the table at his ex-wife, while Frieda watched him with an anxious frown.

"That's the most outrageous thing I've ever seen," Chauncey said more quietly this time. By then, Felicia knew what it was about.

"I don't like it either," Olympia said to Chauncey quietly after he sat down. "She had it done while she was at school. I just discovered it this week."

"You're far too liberal with that child, with all of them in fact. She'll wind up in jail as a Communist one of these days," he said, as he ordered another drink.

"They don't put Communists in jail, Chauncey. She's liberal, but she's not totally out of her mind. She just wants to prove she has her own ideas."

"That's no way to do it," he said with a look of outraged disapproval. Veronica's tattoo had shocked him to the core.

"No, it isn't. I hate to say it, but I suppose it's harmless. Ugly, but harmless." Olympia was resigning herself to something she knew she could do nothing about.

"She's disfigured for the rest of her life." He looked pained, and it was obvious that he blamed Olympia for allowing it to happen. She hadn't, but he blamed her anyway. He always did, and always had.

"She's not disfigured," her mother defended her. "She's still a lovely girl. It was a foolish thing to do. And if she hates it later on, which I hope she will, she can have it removed."

"We should force her to," he said, looking hopeful as he finished his drink.

"No, Chauncey, we shouldn't. She'd just get another one right now. Give it time." He shook his head, and said something under his breath to his wife, and then seemed to notice Frieda for the first time, and decided to vent his spleen on her.

"I suppose your son has tattoos, too," he said accusingly. It had to be someone's fault. In this case Olympia *and* Harry's. Frieda smiled at him, looking vastly amused. He was easy to read. She had dealt with his kind of prejudice for years.

"No, he doesn't. Jews don't get tattoos. They're against our religion."

"Oh," he said, not knowing how to respond. He said something to Felicia then, and they both got up. The meal was over, and it was time to go back upstairs and join their guests in the ballroom. The girls were going to form a receiving line, to greet the guests as they went in, while their escorts waited for them backstage. It was nearly nine o'clock.

Chapter 9

Olympia rolled Frieda toward the elevator after the girls left. When last seen, Veronica had the stole neatly draped over her shoulders, and Olympia was once again grateful that Frieda had made it for her. At least the entire ballroom wasn't going to get a view of her tattoo. The rest of them had seen enough of it during dinner, and it had caused considerable stir.

"I'm sorry about Chauncey," Olympia apologized to her, as she rolled her toward the elevator in the wheelchair.

"It's not your fault. It always amazes me that there are still people like him around. That kind of prejudice still takes me by surprise. He must live in a very sheltered world."

"He does," Olympia assured her, grateful that she was no longer married to him. Whatever Harry's faults, he was an intelligent, kind, decent man.

Once on the ballroom floor again, they went through the receiving line. It seemed to take forever, and Frieda sat and beamed at the girls when they got to them. She and Olympia had shaken all fifty properly extended gloved right hands. There were some very pretty girls in the group, but none as pretty, Olympia thought, as her twins. They looked dazzling in the very different but equally beautiful white evening gowns.

Frieda was still smiling with pride and pleasure when they found their table. Olympia settled her in, and sat down next to her. Ginny's friend Steve was already sitting there. He stood up politely and introduced himself, looking faintly embarrassed, and then sat down again. Olympia was cool and still seriously annoyed at him. The other couple she had invited came shortly afterward. She introduced them to Frieda, and within seconds Margaret Washington and her husband appeared. She had left her mother at the hospital in good hands. She was wearing a spectacular brown lace gown, almost the same color as her skin. Frieda thought she looked like a young Lena Horne. It was a congenial group as everyone talked about how beautiful the girls had looked on the receiving line.

Five minutes later, Chauncey and Felicia arrived. Olympia noticed that Chauncey was beginning to show the vast quantity of booze he had on board. And much to Olympia's annoyance, he stared at Margaret and her husband in disbelief as though he had never seen African Americans before. Or surely not here. He said not a word, looked at Olympia unhappily, and sat down. She had done the unthinkable. She had not only brought a Jewish woman with her to the ball, she had invited an African American couple. Chauncey looked as though he were going to burst an artery. And to add insult to injury, his daughter had a tattoo. Seeing the look on his face, Olympia started to laugh. Margaret's eyes met hers, and registered what she was laughing about, and she started laughing, too. Frieda was smiling blissfully, oblivious to what was going on. She loved watching the people, and seeing the jewels and evening gowns, and the pretty young girls. Frieda thought the ballroom was like something in a fairy tale. The look on her face was worth the entire night to her daughter-in-law. Whatever Chauncey thought of it, she knew she had done the right thing. Frieda deserved to be there as much as anyone else in the room. The days of Chauncey's world, its values and segregated, secluded life were over. In the end, what Olympia had done was far more powerful than Harry's statement by refusing to come. He had done exactly what people like Chauncey wanted, and stayed home. Olympia had brought the real world right into the ball with her, a Holocaust survivor and a brilliant young black lawyer who had grown up in Harlem. What better way to prove the point to them? She could think of none.

As she thought about it, she was startled to see Charlie walk toward her across the ballroom, and wondered if something was wrong. Everyone was at their table by then, and the girls had gone backstage to get ready for the presentation. Noses were being powdered, hair was being smoothed down and combed, lipstick was being put on. The band had begun to play, and the debutantes' parents and friends were dancing. They had another twenty minutes to enjoy themselves before the show began. Charlie strode purposefully across the floor, and much to his mother's surprise, he asked her to dance. She smiled at him, touched by the gesture. She knew he had done it because Harry wasn't there. And he knew how hard it was for her to spend an evening with his father. He had been boorish to her about the tattoo and rude to her guests. And for some odd reason, Chauncey and Felicia had invited none of their own. Charlie led his mother out on the dance floor, among the other parents, and began a graceful fox trot with her.

"Have I told you lately how proud I am of you?" She looked up at her firstborn with a happy smile, while Frieda watched them with pleasure. Olympia was a beautiful woman, and her son was a handsome, kind-hearted boy. He'd been eight when Olympia and Harry got married, and Frieda had watched him grow from child to man. Like his mother, she was proud of him, too. He was a good boy.

"I love you, Mom," Charlie said quietly, and she saw the same shadow in his eyes again, as though there were a question there. No matter how hard she tried, she couldn't figure out the question, or the answer.

"I love you, too, Charlie. More than you know. The girls look pretty tonight, don't they?" He nodded, and she continued chatting as they danced. It had been years since she danced with him. It startled her to realize how much he looked like his father at the same age, but he was a much better person. "There are a lot of pretty girls here tonight. Maybe you'll find the girl of your dreams," she teased him. In truth, she would have been unhappy if he had. She wanted him to find a girl from a more interesting world than this one. These people were all right for one night, but in some ways they were an oddity, a relic from the past, like Charlie's father. She wanted him to find someone with broader horizons than these, a woman whose values weren't as narrow. And as she thought about it, Charlie looked down at her with a quiet smile.

"I know this is a crazy place to do it, Mom. And I know it's probably the wrong time. But I've wanted to tell you something for a while."

"If you tell me you have a skull and crossbones tattooed on your chest, I'm going to hit you." He laughed and shook his head, and his eyes grew serious again.

"No, Mom. I'm gay." He didn't miss a step as he danced with her, and she looked at him with eyes filled with more love and pride than he had ever dared to hope he would see there once he told her. She hadn't let him down. And for her, the question she'd seen in his eyes for so long had finally been answered. She didn't say anything for a long time, and then she leaned closer to him and kissed him.

"I love you, Charlie. Thank you for telling me." His confidence in her was the greatest gift he could have given her, just as her peaceful acceptance of what he had told her was the greatest gift she could have given him. "I guess when I think about it, I'm not all that surprised. I am, but I'm not. Was that what happened with the boy who killed himself last year? Were you in love with him?" Maybe in her heart of hearts she had wondered about it all along. She was no longer sure. Maybe her heart had told her Charlie was different long before her head understood.

"No." He shook his head. "We were just friends. He went home for the weekend and told his parents he was gay, too, and his father said he never wanted to see him again. He killed himself when he got back."

"How terrible of his father to do something like that." She caught a glimpse of Chauncey over his shoulder as they danced. It was not going to be easy for Charlie to share this news with him. They both knew that. Chauncey had a million prejudices on a multitude of subjects.

"I think I was afraid that something like that could happen to me. Not killing myself. But I was afraid of what you'd say if I told you and Dad. I think I knew you'd be okay, but you never know. And I can't see Dad taking it well."

"He probably won't. He has some growing up to do. Maybe I can help. But I don't think you should try telling him tonight," she said cautiously, and Charlie laughed. Chauncey was obviously drunk, as always.

"I wasn't planning to tell him tonight. I've wanted to tell you and Harry for months. Do you think he'll be okay?" Charlie asked with a look of concern. What Harry thought mattered a lot to him. He had deep respect for the man, even though he wasn't there that night. Not being there was just something

Harry thought he had to do. They had all forgiven him by then, even his wife.

"I think Harry will be fine. In fact, I'm sure of it. Tell him whenever you want."

"I will. Thanks, Mom," he said then, looking down at her. He looked happier than she'd seen him in months. And as she looked at him, the dance came to an end. "You're the best mom anyone could ever have. Now can I tell you about the tattoo on my back?" He laughed at her, looking like a kid again. But that night they both knew he had become a man. He had taken the terrifying step from childhood into adulthood. Tonight had been a rite of passage for him, too, a terrifying one. And thanks to her, he had landed on both feet, and the ground under him was solid, whatever his sexual preferences were. She loved him no matter what. That was clear. He had her unconditional love and respect.

"Don't you dare tell me you have a tattoo, Charlie Walker. I might have to strangle you for that!"

"Don't worry, Mom, I don't." He had to go backstage to the others then, but he had known that before he did, he had to tell her. He didn't know why, but he knew that he had to tell her tonight. He wanted to. In a different way than his sisters, he had come out, too.

She turned to look at him again before he led her back to her table, and she told him just what he wanted to hear and needed from her. "I'm proud of you." He kissed her cheek and led her back to her table. There, standing quietly next to her seat, was Harry in white tie and tails, watching her. He looked as though he had always planned to be there with her. Frieda was beaming up at him with pride. It had not just been a night for the girls, it was a good night for sons, too.

"What are you doing here?" she asked softly, smiling at him, as Charlie left them. She was touched beyond words that he was there. His coming, despite his principles and objections, was a gift she would forever cherish, as she would the trust of her son. It had been a memorable night so far.

"I decided to take your suggestion, and my mother's, and get over myself. I thought tonight might be a good time to do it." Everyone seemed to be having epiphanies that night, and she had had hers, too. She realized that she loved him, whether he came to the ball or not. She had given up hoping ever since he told her how strongly he felt about it.

"Do we have time for a dance?" he asked her gently, and she nodded. It was the last dance before the presentation. He had orchestrated his arrival perfectly.

"I love you, Harry," she said happily, waltzing slowly in his arms.

"I love you, too. I'm sorry I was such a pain in the ass over this. I guess I had to work it out for myself." And then he laughed. "My mother told me tonight when she left that she was ashamed of me. She said I was the most prejudiced person she knew. Max even said it was stupid of me not to come. I know it was. The only one I care about here is you, and the kids of course. But I wanted to be here with you. I'm sorry I let you come here alone. How was dinner, by the way?"

"Interesting. Chauncey had a tantrum over Veronica's tattoo. I don't blame him, but as usual, he went a little overboard."

"Did she tell him to get fucked?" he asked with amusement. He had obviously missed the fireworks over dinner, but had turned up for the best part, the part that really mattered to her. The presentation of her girls to society, whatever that was.

"Remarkably, she didn't," she said in answer to his question about what Veronica had said to her father. "She told him to grow up. That's not a bad idea. Getting sober wouldn't be a bad idea, either. He still drinks too much." She had a lot of things to tell him when they went home that night, mostly Charlie's admission to her. It was foremost in her mind. But she didn't want to tell him here. She was still a little startled by what her son had told her, but touched that he had taken her into his confidence at last. He had looked like a thousand-pound weight had been lifted off his shoulders from the moment he told her. She still had to digest it herself. But in the end, whatever he was or wanted or needed, or made him happy, was fine with her. And she knew it would be with Harry, too. Chauncey was another story. She suspected he was going to take longer to adjust. And then she laughed as she continued to fill Harry in on what he'd missed. "I thought Chauncey was going to have a heart attack when the Washingtons walked in." Harry laughed in response.

"You certainly know how to make a statement a lot better than I do. Whatever their rules are, you've probably broken all of them with who you have at your table, along with the biggest WASP in Newport. That's one way to mix it up, and drag these people into the real world. How's my mother doing?"

"I think she's having fun." She smiled up at her husband then, with a look of obvious pleasure. "Thank you for coming, Harry. I'm so glad you're here." He could see how much it meant to her and was pleased. He had done the right thing in the end and he knew it.

"So am I. When does the show begin?" A drumroll at the end of their waltz answered his question, as the bandleader asked everyone to take their seats.

Harry followed his wife off the floor, and sat down next to her and his mother in her wheelchair, and a moment later, the room went dark, a curtain rose, and a spotlight shone on an arch of flowers. A line of cadets from West Point appeared, raised their sabers, and crossed them. The debutantes were going to pass underneath, just as they had when Olympia made her debut twenty-seven years before. Frieda's eyes were wide as she watched the performance, and a moment later, the first girl came out. They appeared alphabetically, and Olympia knew that with the last name of Walker, the twins were going to come out last. They had forty-eight other girls to watch before Virginia and Veronica made their bows.

The girls came out slowly, some looking nervous, others looking confident, some smiling broadly, others not at all. The wreaths of flowers on their heads made them look almost angelic, and some of the gowns were really lovely, others were slightly over the top. There were fat girls and thin ones, exquisite ones and plain ones, but as each of them came out, holding her bouquet, her gloved hand tucked into her escort's arm, each looked as though it was the most glorious moment of her life. The announcer called their names, and those of their escorts. They stood still, as everyone applauded, siblings whistled and shouted, and with measured grace, they curtsied, walked slowly down the stairs and under the cadets' sabers, and crossed the ballroom to wait for the others. There was something slightly silly about it, and wonderfully old-fashioned. It was easy to imagine girls doing it for the past several hundred years, right into modern times. Unlike their ancestors, these girls were no longer looking for husbands. They were stepping out into the world among family and friends for one magical moment they would remember forever. It was a world waiting to receive them and celebrate them, one that would be easy for some and harder for others. But tonight, in this one shining moment, everything that was happening was to assure them that everyone in the room loved them, was proud of them, and wished them well. There was an overwhelming feeling of joy and tender approbation in the room, as everyone applauded for each girl. And then at last, Olympia and those at her table applauded as first Veronica and then Virginia came out. Veronica looked anything but reluctant. She looked confident and proud, smiled a sexy smile, held her stole around her, and came down the stairs with measured steps, passed under the swords, and crossed the room to the others. Then Charlie appeared with Virginia. He looked incredibly dashing as he tucked his sister's gloved hand into his arm. He squeezed her arm gently, as she smiled shyly, dropped into a graceful curtsy, and walked slowly down the stairs and past the cadets. They paraded one more time around the dance floor, stood in a breathtaking line of young beauties, curtsied one last time, and then the fathers were invited to come to the dance floor. Chauncey got up more steadily than Olympia expected, and walked proudly onto the dance floor to claim Virginia. Olympia then whispered something to Harry. He hesitated, and she nodded, and then he went out to claim Veronica.

Chauncey glanced at him for a moment, and then nodded. As though prearranged, they each danced with one girl for half a dance, and then switched. It was a moment Olympia knew that she, Harry, and Frieda would never forget. The man who had objected so strenuously to everything the evening stood for had danced with her daughters the night of their debut. And when the dance was over, much to Olympia's amazement, Chauncey shook his hand. It had turned out to be a rite of passage not only for the children but for the adults as well. Both families had acknowledged their bond to each other through their children. And then Chauncey came back to the table and invited Olympia to dance.

"I still haven't gotten over that tattoo," he said, looking down at her, smiling this time. For an instant, she could almost remember the man she had once loved. He shared these lovely children with her, and they had just shared a night that they would all long remember and cherish. She laughed at what he said.

"Neither have I. I thought I was going to keel over when I saw it. I guess our children will always surprise us, and not always in the ways we want. But we're lucky, Chauncey, they're great kids."

"Yes," he admitted without hesitation, "they are." She looked across the dance floor and saw Harry dancing with Felicia, Veronica with Charlie, and Ginny happily in the arms of Steve, who had broken her heart the night before. She was laughing as he said something to her, and Olympia couldn't help wondering if Ginny had dazzled him and changed his mind that night. She hoped so. The girls deserved to be happy on that night more than all others. She knew that the girls would be out with their friends all night, and home after they had breakfast somewhere.

Both girls made a point of coming over to

her to tell her how much they loved her, and how glad they were that they'd done it. Veronica hugged her extra tight, and all three women cried as the twins thanked her. In that one shining moment, Olympia knew it had all been worthwhile.

She and Harry danced long after Chauncey and Felicia and their guests left. Frieda sat happily in her wheelchair, enjoying the music and watching the people. They all had midnight supper, and it was two in the morning when all three Rubinsteins left. Frieda said that if she hadn't broken her ankle and been in a cast, she would have danced all night. She said it was the most magical evening of her life. Just seeing how thrilled she was to have been there touched Harry's and Olympia's hearts.

Charlie had made a point of coming to say good-bye to them before he left with the girls. They were going to a private club to dance some more. It was a night none of them would ever forget. Charlie had whispered to his mother before he left, "Thanks again, Mom, I love you."

"I love you, too, sweetheart." She smiled at him. For that one night, everything that mattered bonded them to each other. Both girls had come to thank her. Even Veronica said she'd had a great time, which was exactly what Harry said as they left.

"I had a terrific time, Ollie," he said, looking at her tenderly. He loved what she had done for his mother. She had known instinctively how much it meant to Frieda, and nothing in the world could have stopped Olympia from getting her there. Each in their own way, they had all come out that night. Perhaps Harry most of all. He had given up his radical ideals for just a moment, allowed himself to be mellowed, and discovered that it wasn't such a travesty to move in many worlds. Frieda's eyes were still sparkling as they got in the limousine. Tonight Frieda was Cinderella, Olympia had been her fairy godmother. And Harry had turned out to be the handsome prince after all.

The three of them gathered in the kitchen when they got home, where Harry made omelets. Frieda was still wearing her beautiful black velvet dress, as Harry loosened his tie. They sat at the kitchen table, talking about each special moment of the night.

"That was quite a dress Felicia was almost wearing," Harry said as he finished his omelet, and Olympia laughed.

"She suits Chauncey to perfection, better than I did," Olympia said generously. "Maybe Veronica broke the ice with her goofy tattoo. Madame Butterfly. Maybe I should get one, too."

"Don't you dare!" Harry growled at her, looking more handsome than ever to his mother and his wife.

Olympia helped Frieda get into bed, while Harry cleaned up the kitchen. Frieda looked up at her daughter-in-law from her pillows, with stars in her eyes.

"Thank you, Olympia. I had the best time I've ever had."

"Me too," Olympia said honestly. "I'm so happy you and Harry were there."

"He's a good boy," Frieda said proudly. "I'm glad he did the right thing."

"He always does," Olympia said, and kissed her good night, then she turned off the light and left the room. Harry was waiting for her in the hallway outside his mother's room. They walked upstairs hand in hand and quietly closed the door to their bedroom, so they didn't wake Max. The sitter Harry had called at the last minute had left when they got home. She'd been fast asleep in Charlie's room, since it was nearly three. It was almost four when Harry unzipped Olympia's dress and looked at her with pleasure, and then she remembered what she hadn't been able to tell him until then. Her eyes grew serious as she looked at him.

"Charlie told me something very important tonight."

"That he has a tattoo, too?" he teased, and she shook her head. She wasn't sad for Charlie. She had enormous respect for him.

"Charlie came out tonight, too."

"Out of what?" Harry asked, looking confused, and then he understood. It didn't completely surprise him, although he had never been sure. But he had wondered once or twice, and didn't want to say anything to Olympia, in case his suspicions weren't accurate. He was afraid it might upset her. It hadn't. It had surprised her, but she loved him more than ever.

"He told me," she said proudly. She was touched by the faith he had put in her. "When we were dancing, right before you got there."

"I wondered what he was saying to you. I was watching you while you danced with him. You looked beautiful." He came to put his arms around her then. "Are you okay with it?" He looked concerned. It was a big admission for her son to make, with many ramifications that would affect him and all of them for years. For the rest of his life.

"I think I am. I just want him to be happy. He looked a lot happier once he told me than he has in a long time."

"Then I'm glad. And relieved for both of you. You know," he said as he sat down on their bed and looked at her. "You were right. I think a coming-out party is a good thing. It's a lot like a bat mitzvah. It's one of those times that makes everybody feel good, not just the girls, but all their friends and families, and everyone who shares it with them. I loved seeing my mom there. And I loved dancing with you and the girls. And stupid as it sounds, when Chauncey shook my hand on the dance floor, it brought tears to my eyes."

There had been tears in his eyes several times that night, and in hers. It had been a night of love and celebration, a night of hope and remembrance, a night when girls became women, children became adults, and strangers became friends. Just as she had said it would be, it was a rite of passage, and a lovely tradition, and nothing more. It was a night when he had come out from an old world into a new one, when others got a glimpse backward into an old one. When the past and future met in one shining moment, when time stopped, sadness slipped away and was forgotten, and life began.